The Choice

A Holocaust Remembrance Book for Young Readers

The CHOICE

Kathy Clark

Second Story Press

Library and Archives Canada Cataloguing in Publication

Clark, Kathy, 1953-, author
The choice / by Kathy Clark.

(The Holocaust remembrance series for young readers)
Issued in print and electronic formats.
ISBN 978-1-927583-65-4 (pbk.).—ISBN 978-1-927583-70-8 (epub)

1. Holocaust, Jewish (1939-1945)—Juvenile fiction. I. Title.
II. Series: Holocaust remembrance book for young readers

PS8555.L3703C46 2015   jC813'.6   C2014-908149-9

C2014-908150-2

Editor: Sarah Swartz
Copyeditor: Karen Helm
Designer: Melissa Kaita

Printed and bound in Canada

*The views or opinons expressed in this book and the context in which the
images are used, do not necessarily reflect the views or policy of, nor imply
approval or endorsement by, the United States Holocaust Memorial Museum.*

*Second Story Press gratefully acknowledges the support of the Ontario Arts Council
and the Canada Council for the Arts for our publishing program. We acknowledge the
financial support of the Government of Canada through the Canada Book Fund.*

Published by
SECOND STORY PRESS
20 Maud Street, Suite 401
Toronto, ON M5V 2M5
www.secondstorypress.ca

To the memory of Frigyes Porscht

Introduction

Hungary was one of the last countries to be assaulted by the Nazi German army during World War II. It was invaded on March 19, 1944, and liberated by the Allies just over a year later during April 1945. Yet within that year about 550,000 Jewish people were killed by the Nazis.

Two circumstances enabled the Nazis to be so successful in their murderous campaign. The first was that many Jews in Hungary were unprepared for the sudden brutality that erupted around them with the Nazi invasion. From the beginning of World War II in 1939 until the invasion by Hitler in March 1944, a span of about five years, the Jews of Hungary led relatively normal lives. While several laws were passed in Hungary during this time – laws that restricted where Jews could work and even whom they could marry – most Jews believed that what was happening in other parts of Europe would never happen

For most of World War II, Hungary remained untouched and its capital, Budapest, set on the Danube River, was as impressive then as it appears today.

in Hungary. Jews in other European countries were rounded up, forced to live in ghettos, or deported to concentration camps where they were starved and forced to work under horrific conditions, or murdered outright in the death camps. By comparison, the Jews of Hungary felt relatively safe. Those things would never happen here, they told themselves. They were wrong.

The reality was that many (though not all) people in Hungary sided with the Nazis. They formed a political party called the Arrow Cross, which modeled itself very closely on the Nazi Party of Germany. Like the Nazis, members of the Arrow Cross considered themselves to be "superior" and believed that the "strongest" people should rule over others. Prior to the Nazi invasion, the party was not officially recognized and had to operate in secret. However, shortly after the German occupation of Hungary in March 1944, the Arrow Cross became the governing body of the country. With the party's rise to power, the lives of all Jews, Roma (or Gypsies as they were called then), and several other minority groups were immediately in danger.

With the full support and co-operation of the Arrow Cross, the German elite military force, called the SS, was able to effectively deport or kill thousands of Jews and impose severe restrictions on their lives. The SS, whose members believed themselves superior in racial purity and ability to the rest of the German army, had its own rank structure and uniforms. Its leader was Heinrich Himmler, and under him the

SS was responsible for establishing and operating concentration camps and death camps in Europe, where millions of people were killed.

One of the largest of these concentration camps was Auschwitz, in Poland. It was actually a network of concentration and death camps with more than forty satellite camps. Most of the Jews deported from Hungary after the German invasion were taken to Auschwitz. While conditions varied slightly from camp to camp, in all of them the prisoners were crowded into barracks, given little food, and forced to perform hard labor. Due to the extremely poor living conditions, many prisoners died of starvation and disease. Others were immediately sent to their deaths upon arrival.

This is the story of a thirteen-year-old boy who lived in Budapest, Hungary, during the turbulent years of World War II. It was a difficult time to be growing up and to take one's place as a young adult in such a confusing and divided country.

November 5, 1944

He huddled in the corner of the crowded freight car. His knees were tight against his chest, his face buried in his hands. He did not notice the oppressive heat, the stench, or the anguished cries of the people pressed tightly against him. He was convinced that the terrible mistakes he had made were written all over his face. Yet, except for the occasional accidental kick or shove, no one seemed to pay him much heed. Everyone was caught up in their own terror. Still, guilt and shame dulled his senses. Even when the train lurched forward and started on its slow journey toward the undisclosed yet ominous destination, he remained immobile, lost in his private nightmare. How could he have been so stupid? Just this morning he had prided himself on finally acting like a man. Now he knew that he had simply behaved like the very foolish thirteen-year-old boy that he was.

What have I done? he asked himself over and over again.

It was only a week ago that the plans had started to take shape in the boy's mind. With each passing day, he had taken daring steps closer to revisiting the life and the loved ones he had been forced to erase from his memory six years earlier. But instead of the positive outcome he had anticipated, his efforts had brought him here – to this train of horrors with nothing but regrets as his companion.

PART
ONE

Chapter 1

October 30, 1944

The idea had first come to Hendrik in Brother Ferenc's religion class, his knees touching those of his best friend, Ivan, beneath the surface of the wooden desk they shared. They were sitting in the ancient yet well-preserved school building, adjacent to the equally old Franciscan monastery. Hendrik glanced through the tall, narrow window at the gnarled stand of oaks that lined the eastern slope of the Sashegy (Eagle Mountain) district of Budapest. He and Ivan and the other boys had climbed those trees numerous times. To them it was as vital a part of their formation as the education they received at the hands of the Franciscan brothers at the elite Assisi School for boys.

"All of you already are or will be thirteen years old at some point during this school year, and it is time for you to begin your preparation for the sacrament of confirmation." The friar's voice boomed over the heads of the neat rows of boys sitting in front of him. Brother Ferenc was a slight man, his back bent with age. The rough brown cloth of the Franciscan friars hung loosely over his shoulders. The strength of his voice contrasted with his frail physical appearance. Vitality radiated from his small gray eyes and wisdom from his words – which always commanded attention and respect.

"Confirmation is your gateway to manhood." Brother Ferenc paused and gave a meaningful glance around the room.

Hendrik and Ivan nudged each other and exchanged a quick smile. To be considered men as soon as possible had been their aim for the last several months – ever since the arrival of the German Nazis in Budapest that March.

Many people in the country referred to that arrival as an invasion by the Nazis and their followers. But some were happy about the change – like those in the Hungarian Arrow Cross Party. The previous government of Hungary had been overthrown, and in its stead the Arrow Cross had been given full power over the country. They imposed their rules – imposed them mainly on the Jewish population of the city, whose rights were suddenly greatly limited. All Jews now had to wear a yellow star whenever they were on the streets. They were forced to live in specially designated buildings or in the newly erected Jewish ghetto. Most of their belongings had been confiscated. Jewish children could no longer attend schools. Jewish stores and businesses had been closed or taken over by others. There were even rumors that many Jews were being deported to concentration camps, driven out of the country by force, and killed.

Hendrik mostly tried to ignore these events, pushing the threat to the Jews into the far recesses of his mind. He had many other secret thoughts and memories hidden there. Ignoring what was happening with the Jews wasn't all that difficult for him. He had never actually witnessed any of the incidents reported in the papers or on the radio. He and his family now lived on the Buda side of the Danube River, far from the Jewish quarter of Pest. What was of more pressing importance to Hendrik was maintaining his friendship with Ivan and their current project of strengthening their bodies.

For Ivan and his family, the German occupation was a welcome turn of events. Ivan's father had been a longtime member of the underground Arrow Cross, formerly outlawed. Now that the Arrow Cross was in power, he was officially promoted to the rank of Sergeant. As Ivan's best friend, Hendrik had been swept up in the excitement of change. He pushed aside all thoughts of what this change really meant.

"We'll exercise so that we will be like real grown-up men. We will become the youngest members of the Arrow Cross," Ivan had plotted. And Hendrik, wanting to please his friend, had joined in the challenge to build up his muscles. Besides, if he started looking more like a man, Father might start to take him more seriously. He might listen to Hendrik's questions and finally trust him with the answers he sought.

Throughout the summer break, he and Ivan had trained daily. They'd run long distances to strengthen their legs. They'd hauled coal, lifted sacks of potatoes, moved bricks at the brickyard. They'd performed any task that guaranteed to build their muscles.

"Soon they will let us wear uniforms, carry guns, patrol the streets and maybe even attack the enemy," Ivan would say with great enthusiasm. Who the enemy was didn't concern them at the moment. The world was at war, soldiers were everywhere, arrests were made daily. There was a growing need for men to join up and fight.

Hendrik enjoyed the challenge of becoming more muscular and athletic – of becoming a man. And he could see that all their hard work was paying off. By the end of the summer, he and Ivan were the tallest, most developed boys in their class. They told themselves that they could easily pass for fifteen- or even sixteen-year-olds.

It had surprised Hendrik at first that a boy like Ivan would befriend him. The day after his family had moved into their new apartment at the base of the Eagle Mountain district of Buda five years earlier, Ivan had come knocking. "I live right across the courtyard," Ivan had said. "I saw you arrive yesterday. I'm going to climb around the block in the treetops today, without once touching the ground. Do you want to come?"

For a moment Hendrik had been too stunned to say anything in response to this unusual invitation. He himself would never have dreamt of inviting someone he didn't know on any sort of excursion, let alone on such an outlandish one. He had always felt safer, more comfortable, staying sheltered in the arms of a soft easy chair, lost inside the pages of a book.

However, with the move to Buda everything in his life had become unpredictable. Plus, he was captivated by Ivan's mischievous smile, his sparkling blue eyes and straw-blond hair, such a sharp contrast to his own dark curls and brown eyes. After a moment's consideration, he had nodded. "You can be Mowgli, the boy, and I'll be Bagheera, the panther. We can pretend we're chasing each other through the jungle." Hendrik had just finished reading the Hungarian translation of *The Jungle Book* by Rudyard Kipling. His mind was still filled with images of a boy living with wild animals.

"Sure," beamed Ivan, "that will make it so much more fun!"

Once outside, Hendrik discovered that Ivan's plan could be achieved more easily than he had anticipated. On their street, lined with ancient chestnuts and sycamores, their thick limbs crisscrossing each other, climbing from one tree to the next was an exciting adventure. After that, Ivan came knocking early each morning with a new proposal. He led the way and Hendrik, finding another suitable story in which to insert their adventure, followed. From that first day in the treetops, the two of them had been inseparable. Spending time with Ivan during the days had made it easier for Hendrik to forget the faces and names that haunted him at night. It got him out of the house, far from his mother's sad eyes and trembling lips. It kept

Budapest was a beautiful city before the war. Hendrik and Ivan's street was lined with ancient chestnut trees, like the ones blooming here. Graceful bridges across the Danube River joined Buda to Pest.

him out of the range of his father's stern gaze, reminding him with every glance what he should and should not say and do. It prevented him from hearing the heavy sighs of their live-in maid, Magda, as she went about her chores. Ivan had helped Hendrik to make the transition from one life to another.

Besides, Hendrik could see that Father approved of the friendship, encouraged it even. "So, what are you two boys up to today?" Father would ask cheerfully as he adjusted his tie and stiffly starched collar before the mirror in the morning. At the end of the day, he would often bring home a chocolate bar or a small bag of sour candies.

"Go share it with your friend," he'd suggest, "and don't forget to pass on my regards to his father." Ivan's father was a man with authority in Budapest. He had been with the Arrow Cross since its inception. It seemed to please Father that Hendrik's friend was the son of such a prominent citizen.

As instructed, Hendrik always took Father's treats to share, but he could never bring himself to pass on Father's message. There was something about the penetrating eyes of Ivan's father that frightened Hendrik.

Chapter 2

"At your confirmation," Brother Ferenc continued, "you will accept the responsibility for your own religious formation and affirm your faith – to God, to your community, and to yourselves. When you were a child, your parents made the decisions for you. They had you baptized into the Catholic church. Until now, the responsibility to raise you in the faith was theirs. Now when you are confirmed, the choice will be yours." It seemed to Hendrik that Brother Ferenc looked pointedly at him as he said those words. For a brief moment their eyes locked.

Your parents made the decisions for you. The choice will be yours.... That look, those words jolted Hendrik like a bolt of lightning. *Does he know about me?* wondered Hendrik.

A strange mixture of fear and longing suddenly gripped Hendrik's heart. His throat constricted and he could barely swallow. A host of forbidden memories burst into his consciousness. He had managed to seal those memories behind an impenetrable wall. Father had made the decision several years ago – a decision Hendrik's young mind had not understood. That he still did not understand.

Now, the choice will be yours. The words echoed over and over in Hendrik's mind, taunting him, daring him to accept the challenge.

For the first time in five years, he allowed himself to remember. He became oblivious to Brother Ferenc's words as he was transported back in time to his earlier childhood. He could picture their spacious apartment on the Pest side of the city across the river, just a few blocks from the entrance onto Margit Bridge. He remembered the sun's rays slanting in through the louvered shutters, casting lines of shadow and light on the pages of his book as he snuggled in his favorite spot beside the large, ceramic-tiled fireplace. He remembered Mother's lighthearted singing as it floated in from the kitchen where she helped Magda prepare their evening meal. He remembered Father relaxed, leaning back in the large, comfortable easy chair, the newspaper spread wide before him, his brown leather briefcase as always by his feet, telling Mother about his day and his latest business dealings.

He remembered the lighting of the candles on Fridays at dusk, just when the shadows lengthened, veiling the corners of the room in mystery. He could sense the flickering flames, the sweet smell of the wax curling high with the smoke. He remembered the family gatherings with his aunt Mimi, his uncle Peter, and his two cousins.

Cousin Lilly was the same age as he and cousin Gabor was five years older. He imagined them around the table laden with steaming trays of brisket, roast potatoes, and sweet compote. He could almost hear again the joking, the laughter, and the love that flowed about the room and bound them together.

And he remembered Aunt Mimi's home just a block from theirs, her welcoming smile when he would arrive on a cold winter's day fresh from tobogganing with Lilly, the tantalizing aroma of hot cocoa and sweet rolls fresh from the oven awaiting them. He remembered Lilly's laughing eyes, her relentless teasing, and her sincere contrition whenever she realized that she had gone too far.

He remembered Gabor, whom he had always admired. Gabor, who had been his hero, showing him how to fashion a slingshot out of a forked stick and coming to his defense at the park whenever he was bullied by older boys. Gabor had convinced him so long ago to abandon his tricycle for the shiny red two-wheeler that Father had bought him. Gabor at thirteen, proudly talking about the bar mitzvah ceremony that would soon take place marking *his* passage into manhood.

Hendrik remembered when the troubles began back in 1939 when he was eight years old. He remembered the crisp, early spring morning when Uncle Peter was ordered to leave Budapest – to work in a forced labor camp. Uncle Peter had embraced them all and then turned to head out the door, his shoulders hunched as if carrying a heavy burden even though his hands were empty. It was shortly after that day that Father came home and announced that they were not going to wait for things to get worse. He wasn't going to be told by the authorities what he could and could not do. No. That day he had begun to set things in progress that would change their lives forever.

All those images clamored for Hendrik's attention at once. And with them, the questions: Why had Father forced them to leave their first home? Why could they no longer visit his aunt and cousins? Why was he forbidden any mention of the past?

And ultimately, the question Brother Ferenc suggested he was now old enough to ask: Had Father made the right decision? Would he, Hendrik, have chosen differently?

Chapter 3

Hendrik knew that he would have to find out the answer to his questions – though not from Father or Mother or even Magda. Experience had taught him that they would refuse to even listen to such questions, let alone answer them. On that first night in their new home, toward the end of the summer of 1939, Father had tried to explain. He had followed Hendrik to his new room and sat with him on his new bed. Everything had felt strange and uncomfortable to the eight-year-old who had left behind all that he had known and loved. That morning they had walked out of their old apartment in Pest as if they were going on one of their regular picnics in the hills of Buda. They never returned.

"Hendrik," Father had begun, the new name sounding awkward on his tongue. "It will take all of us a while till we become accustomed to all these changes. I know that it must be difficult for you to understand. But there is a major war looming over Europe and the lives of the Jewish people are threatened. A few months ago, throughout Germany and Austria, the homes and stores of thousands of Jews were vandalized and destroyed. Many people were killed. Others were carted off to prison camps. Even here in Hungary, in order not to displease the Nazis, people like Uncle Peter have been sent to labor camps. I cannot sit by and wait until even worse things happen here. I am responsible for our safety and for ensuring not only that we live, but that we live well. Sadly," Father continued, "I cannot save everyone I love. My first responsibility is for you and your mother."

He ran his fingers gently through Hendrik's curls. "There is one thing I must insist upon from this moment," and he tilted Hendrik's face up and looked directly into his eyes. Suddenly, Father's voice became more stern than Hendrik had ever heard it before. "You must never, never speak of our past lives. Not to anyone else and not even among ourselves. No one must know who we are, that we are Jewish. It is too dangerous. These days even the walls have ears. A wrong word or name dropped carelessly into a conversation can cause people to ask questions. Everything I've tried so hard to achieve could unravel and our lives could be at risk. Do you understand? Your mother and I, you, even Magda – we could all be killed. Your past does not exist. We are starting a brand-new life. We are Catholics now and, as far as everyone will know, we always were. It is because of this that you must never mention your aunt and cousins again. Never!"

Hendrik had not understood – especially why he could not see his aunt and cousins. But he did understand Father's fear and that he must obey. He promised never to breathe a word about their past as Jews. Not to anyone.

Father had hugged him to his chest then and kissed the top of his head. "With time, it will get easier, you'll see. You are young. You will soon forget that you ever had a life different from the one we are starting now. And when you are older, you will understand."

And the next morning Ivan had arrived at their door. Suddenly Father's words from the night before were made true. With Ivan's presence, forgetting the past did become easier.

But today, here in the classroom, Hendrik knew that he would have to break his promise to his father. Now it was time for him to understand for himself why they had left everything behind. He needed to find Aunt Mimi, Gabor, and Lilly and talk with them. They were the key to his past. They would help him to find the answers he sought. Hendrik's heart thumped faster as he considered seeing them again. He hadn't realized how much he missed his aunt and cousins, and the warmth and laughter that his own home once had. He grimaced desperately trying to keep away his tears.

A sharp nudge in his side from Ivan refocused Hendrik's attention to the classroom.

"What's the matter?" Ivan whispered. Hendrik stared at him, wondering if he might have let something slip. He swiped angrily at his eyes.

"It's nothing. Just a bad cramp in my calf," he lied, stretching his leg. Cramps were a common occurrence these days with their heavy exercise routine.

But it was almost impossible now to think about anything other than his past life. A life that had suddenly intruded into the present and felt more real than the hard surface of the desk his hands rested on. And the thought of visiting his aunt and cousins – of choosing for himself as Brother Ferenc had suggested – was dizzying. The memory of Father's stern voice and the severe look in his eyes when he first gave his command still made Hendrik tremble. *Your past does not exist. We are starting a brand-new life. You must never mention your aunt and cousins again. Never!*

For a while, every night at bedtime, Father had quizzed him about what he and Ivan had done and what they had talked about. Hendrik knew it was in order to make sure that he kept to his vow of silence. It was weeks before Father relaxed – assured that Hendrik was following his instructions and blocking out the past.

Keeping his promise to his father, he had never told Ivan the truth about his previous life. How was he going to explain all this to Ivan now after so many years of silence? He wanted Ivan to accompany him on his visit to his aunt and cousins. It would be another adventure and Hendrik couldn't imagine doing anything quite so daring by himself. Would Ivan understand that he was forced to keep his true past a secret? *I couldn't* or *I forgot* seemed lame and false, even though it was the truth.

Hendrik had to admit there had been opportunities to reveal his secret over the last few years. This was especially the case more recently since the Nazi invasion. But each time, Hendrik had pulled back, fearful of losing Ivan's friendship or of having to deal with Father's anger.

Shortly before the current school term started, he had overheard the tail end of an argument between Mother and Father. "We have to talk with him," Mother's voice had been urgent. "We can't let him continue like this. Soon he will be actually able to join the Arrow Cross. We can't let him take that step."

"No. We must wait," Father had insisted. "It would be more dangerous now than ever to be found out. We are fortunate that our son has adapted so well. His friendship with Ivan has been a great help. We mustn't say anything until it is absolutely necessary."

Ivan will understand, when I tell him the truth, Hendrik reassured himself now. *Isn't that what best friends do? Don't they stand by each other, no matter what?*

Hendrik wrestled with whether or not to tell Ivan as they made their way home along the cobblestone streets. As usual, Ivan, the more talkative of the two, chatted about their various classes, the friars who taught them, and the bits of gossip he had overheard. He seemed not to notice that Hendrik was quieter than usual, that his attention was focused elsewhere. When they parted, Hendrik had still not said anything of the turmoil that raged in his mind and heart.

That evening at the dinner table, as Father and Mother questioned him about his school day, he mentioned the upcoming confirmation ceremony and the in-depth studies of the Catholic faith that they were to begin in Brother Ferenc's class.

He held his breath as he waited for Father's response. There was only a moment of uncertain silence. An almost indiscernible glance exchanged between Mother and Father.

"That's wonderful!" Father said, his voice light, in strange contrast to the fierce look he fixed upon Hendrik. "You will be officially a man. We will have to have a big celebration. They will need to see your baptismal certificate. I have it in my desk and will give it to you after dinner." He pretended to smile but his eyes were troubled as he ended the conversation.

"I will bring our dessert," Mother said, rising. "Magda made your favorite crepe torte, Hendrik." She turned toward the kitchen then, but not before Hendrik noticed the slight tremor of her chin.

Chapter 4

Hendrik tossed and turned all night, his dreams filled with a jumble of shadowy forms. People eluded him as he chased them down one street after another. He, himself, was fleeing some unknown menace that was slowly gaining ground. Hendrik woke up feeling groggy and stumbled down the stairs to meet Ivan in the courtyard. The instant they met, Ivan burst out with his own exciting news.

"Guess what? Father said that this Saturday I can go with him while he inspects the patrols in various neighborhoods of the city. He said he might even find me a uniform to wear so that I look more official. I've grown so much and my shoulders are broadening out, so I could easily fit into a man's jacket."

Hendrik tried to share Ivan's enthusiasm. But suddenly there was a nagging unease at the back of his mind. He could no longer ignore that this was about joining the Arrow Cross. Still, Ivan was his best friend, so Hendrik waited for Ivan to invite him to come along, as he usually did.

This time, however, there was no invitation. Not even a wistful *I wish you could come too.* It became clear that in his excitement Ivan had forgotten all about him. Hendrik's thoughts of revealing his past and sharing his future plans faded.

Yes, it was better that Ivan didn't know. Better to wait, to go back on his own, to see what he could find, and then tell Ivan. They didn't have to do *everything* together. Perhaps it was a good coincidence that Ivan would be so thoroughly engaged on Saturday, and not giving a single thought to how Hendrik would be spending his time. Hendrik suddenly felt light-headed, almost giddy, at the thought of doing something important on his own. It would be his first truly independent act – just like a man.

Over the next few days, he listened more attentively to the news on the radio and read more than just the headlines in the newspaper. He eavesdropped on Mother and Magda's hushed conversations. Unseen, he lifted a few food items from their well-stocked pantry. By Saturday morning he was ready.

"I'm doing research for a school assignment and one of the brothers told us about a book dealer who has a stack of old maps. I'm going to go look at them," he told a well-rehearsed half-truth. Then he pedaled rapidly out of the courtyard, ignoring Magda's shrill voice calling after him asking the whereabouts of the dealer. He was free, confident of success and buoyed by the thrill of secrecy and adventure.

Rounding the corner of his apartment building, he came face to face with an Arrow Cross soldier. "Good morning, Sergeant Balint," Hendrik saluted him as was his habit.

"Good morning, Hendrik," the sergeant smiled at him. "Where are you off to so early on a Saturday morning?"

"I'm going over to Pest to a special book dealer's shop. I'm looking for books to complete a school assignment." The excuse flowed easier with each repetition.

"And where's your other half? Where is Ivan? It's rare to see one of you without the other."

"He's spending the day with his father. I wish I were his brother so that I could have gone too," Hendrik said, purposefully allowing the surge of disappointment he had felt to wash over him again.

"Well, your day will come soon enough. Just look at those muscles on you." Sergeant Balint squeezed Hendrik's biceps. "You'll be one of us in no time." There was no request to produce the identification papers that everyone had to carry with them these days or to have his knapsack examined. Hendrik had counted on this familiarity with the soldiers patrolling his immediate neighborhood, both the Nazi SS and the Hungarian Arrow Cross. For now, the assortment of pilfered food concealed beneath his textbooks was safe. He hoped he would be able to get by the patrols on the bridge at the Pest side of the Danube as easily.

Ivan's father was a proud member
of the Arrow Cross and Ivan
longed to wear the uniform too,
and join his father on patrols.

Chapter 5

Hendrik wove his way down the winding tree-lined side streets of Buda to the Danube River, crisscrossing the busy main street several times in an attempt to stay clear of streetcars, trolley buses, and army vehicles. The return trip home, pedaling uphill most of the way, would not be quite as easy. It was a crisp October day, and though the sun's rays filtered through the yellowing leaves, Hendrik was glad of the extra sweater he had pulled over his head just before he left. As he cycled, he kept a running list in his head of things he must remember to tell Ivan the following day when they would exchange notes on their activities. Whether or not he told Ivan the true nature of his trip, he would certainly tell him about his bike ride over to Pest. He wanted to make it sound as exciting as possible.

When he arrived at the bottom of Gellert Mountain, Hendrik turned left onto the ramparts bordering the Danube. High above him, he could just discern the black mouths of canons poking out from the heavily fortified Nazi army base. Over the centuries, the citadel on top of Gellert Mountain, with its wide panoramic view of both sides of the river, had been used by other invading armies in attempts to control the city.

To his right, the river, a wide expanse of grayish-blue water, was teeming with both military and freight ships. How different it looked now from that lazy Sunday afternoon two years ago, when he and Father and Mother had drifted down past Margit Island on an elegant tour boat. They had enjoyed the gentle breeze off the water as they dined and listened to the orchestra performing a medley of classical music. It had been one of those rare days when they had managed to shake off the fears that had been their constant companion ever since their move from across the river.

Hendrik now tensed as he approached the entrance to Erzsebet Bridge. The soldiers keeping guard here were strangers, their red and white striped armbands with the black, pointed arrow cross menacing in the glaring sun. Just a few days ago he wouldn't have given them a second's thought; now, everything had changed. Hendrik straightened his back and forced himself to whistle a lighthearted tune. Again he gave his customary salute as he sped by, counting on his feigned confidence to gain ready access both onto and off the bridge. He passed the first set of guards without incident. But as he neared the Pest side of the river, a soldier blocked his path.

"Papers!" the order rang out. Hendrik fumbled in his pockets, almost tearing the important documents with his nervous fingers. The Arrow Cross soldier, who Hendrik figured was probably only a few years older than he was, seemed to scrutinize every word. *What's the matter? Can't you read?* Hendrik was tempted to ask. But he held his tongue. Ivan would have been able to think of some clever comeback had he been there.

"Open up!" the soldier prodded Hendrik's knapsack with the barrel of his gun after returning the identification papers.

Hendrik was about to answer, when another, older soldier who had been observing them from a distance sauntered over.

"Let him go," he said dismissively. "He's only a boy. No point in wasting time on him. Let's take care of that group of Jews we've rounded up over there. That should be more entertaining." They both chuckled and turned away from Hendrik, who exhaled a sigh of relief. As he sped off on his bicycle, a volley of gunshots erupted behind him.

When he entered the busy streets of Pest, Hendrik slowed his pace. How different it was from where he lived now in Buda. The flat terrain, the tall buildings, the streets congested with traffic and people, and the air heavy with the mingled odor of diesel fuel and cooking made Hendrik feel as though he had traveled to a foreign land. Forbidden by Father, he had not ventured over to this side of the river since their move five years ago. He wound his way carefully along the narrow streets branching off the main avenue.

Gradually, the once-familiar sights evoked more long-buried memories. Here was the street corner where he had gotten into a fight. There was the bakery where Father had bought fresh crescent rolls early each morning and challah every Friday afternoon on his way home from work. Just down the next block would be the coffee shop where Mother liked to stop for her afternoon espresso, always sharing with Hendrik one of the many pastries on display in the window. Around the corner, the large public school Hendrik used to attend occupied the entire block. He recalled the noisy corridors jostling with rambunctious boys, the dusty playground with its chicken-wire partition separating the boys from the girls. He looked with fondness at the solid soot-covered buildings around him; the last five years dissolved and he was once again a small boy, familiar with every nook and alleyway of his neighborhood.

Yet he quickly noticed that not all was as it used to be. Several of the residential buildings had large yellow stars attached above their main entrances. Some storefront windows were boarded up. And he could tell by looking at the shop signs that other businesses once owned by Jews now had different owners. He pulled up sharply as he came to the coffee shop. A sign now hung in its window: *No Jews Allowed.*

Hendrik shuddered. He kept his head low as he continued on his way, and turned up the collar of his shirt. He wished he had thought of wearing a cap to help conceal his face. What if someone recognized him after all these years and called out his name?

But his good fortune continued. He found the bookstore that had served as his excuse to Magda, and stepped inside briefly. Easing his sense of guilt for lying to the housekeeper, he browsed without actually seeing the books on the shelves. Then he left.

A few blocks past the store, he came to the ghetto wall.

Chapter 6

The construction of the ghetto wall to hold in the Jews had begun just that week. Hendrik had heard it announced on the radio. He knew, however, that many people had been forced to move into the area weeks earlier. He had heard Mother's and Magda's hushed voices behind the kitchen door one day in September, shortly after school had started. His mind had locked away the few words that drifted in to him through the half-closed door.

"Today I went to where the Nazis are building the walls of the ghetto," Magda had whispered furtively. "I knew you wouldn't be able to rest till you knew your family was still safe. They're among the more fortunate ones. Though they were forced out of their home, they at least have another place to live, even if it is crowded with several other families in the same apartment. It's above the cobbler's on Kiraly Street. I took them some food."

Hendrik was grateful for those snatches of information. Magda's words were now his only guide. Carefully weaving in and out of the traffic of horse-drawn carts, streetcars, and lumbering army trucks, he circled the wall searching for a safe point of entry. In some places the buildings themselves – their front entrances sealed shut with bricks – formed the wall. In others, the wall was still under construction, while over several blocks it was already several meters high. There were many more soldiers here – both Arrow Cross and Nazi – patrolling the streets and checking identification papers. Where it was complete, the wall was taller than Hendrik had anticipated, made of various-sized stones laid one on top of the other, secured at the top.

The few openings that allowed for the limited movement of people and goods were heavily guarded. Though he had official papers with his false Christian identity, Hendrik wanted to avoid entering the ghetto through one of the guarded gates. His knapsack was sure to be searched this time. He might be asked uncomfortable questions. While coming up with an excuse for his excursion for Magda and his parents was easy, he was terrified of having to make up a story justifying his entry into the ghetto area.

Hendrik soon found what he was looking for. Near the secluded corner of Cseny and Kiraly streets was an old oak, the large brown-leafed limbs of which extended to the other side of the wall. Hendrik dismounted and leaned his bicycle against the gnarled trunk, then eyed the tree for a few moments. He glanced up and down the street, making sure that the coast was clear. Spitting on both his palms, he rubbed his hands together for a better grip, then jumped. He just barely managed to grab hold of the lowest bough. Kicking his legs in order to gain added height and momentum, he hauled himself onto the branch. He stood quickly and climbed higher into the safety of the foliage before any passerby might notice him. In seconds, he reached the branch that hung its weathered acorns into the ghetto then eased forward.

If only Ivan was here, he thought, suddenly missing his friend. This was just the kind of adventure that Ivan would relish. *We would pretend to be Robin Hood of Locksley and Little John, sneaking into the king's fortified palace to free the prisoners.* Except that this wasn't like one of those fabricated adventures of the past. This was for real, with real dangers.

Hendrik took a deep breath. Seeing that the coast was clear, he dropped first his knapsack, then himself, to the ground.

Chapter 7

It took Hendrik a few moments to orient himself. He was startled by the drastic transformation that had taken place on this side of the wall. It had also been a long time since he had been here. He had been a small child then and not overly observant of his neighborhood. The sidewalk was strewn with garbage and a foul smell accosted his nostrils. As he walked to the far corner to read the road sign, he passed a heap of rumpled rags near the front step of a shop. He jumped as the rags moaned. The rags concealed the body of a frail woman.

Hendrik hesitated. Was there anything he could do to help this woman? As he stood there unable to make up his mind, a small group of men came toward him. They were bent and haggard, and their soiled, wrinkled jackets hung limply from their shoulders, each one affixed with a large yellow star. They barely glanced at the woman on the ground. Hendrik was more of a curiosity to them: they eyed his fit body and immaculate clothing with envy. Suddenly fearful, he grabbed a firm hold of his knapsack and hurried on, forgetting about the woman on the ground.

He discovered that the streets were littered with people hunched in doorways, begging at street corners. Their bodies looked emaciated by hunger and disease. There was no way he could help. The farther he walked, the more bewildered he became. Until now, the ghetto had been nothing more than a guarded wall near his old neighborhood to him. The news reports he had heard on the radio had made no mention of the conditions inside. For the first time, it occurred to Hendrik that perhaps the announcers chose the fragments of truth that they wanted revealed. He wondered if Ivan knew from his father about the reality of life on the other side of the walls.

Several people wove their way aimlessly around their less fortunate neighbors. But they too were like the group of men who had passed Hendrik a few moments before. All wore the designated yellow star pinned to their clothing and had vacant, desperate looks in their eyes. He was keenly aware that the yellow star was conspicuously absent from his own sweater. The children he saw seemed listless as well, too weak from hunger to run or play, or even to cry. Over and over, Hendrik was tempted to reach into his knapsack and offer an apple or a hunk of bread. But each time he reminded himself of where he was headed and saved his treasures for those he loved.

At last he arrived at a street corner he recognized. The small store with its window display of handmade bears, dolls, and toy soldiers had been his favorite when he was a small boy. The window display hadn't changed much over the years, but the red wooden door leading into the store was now bolted shut and a sign saying "Keep Out" was nailed on it. Hendrik knew that the cobbler's, above which Aunt Mimi now lived, would be straight ahead and to the right. He pressed on, ever more conscious of the squalor around him. When he reached the building, he had to ask directions to find his aunt's apartment. People appeared to be confused as to who lived exactly where.

He knocked on the door, but no one answered. When he pushed open the unlocked door and stepped inside, he understood why. There were many people, probably three or more families, cramped inside one small room. The sofa and chairs were occupied by the most elderly in the group. Several men and children were sprawled on the bare floor. Aunt Mimi stood, leaning against the doorjamb leading to the kitchen. Hendrik immediately recognized her distinctive head of red curls. A hush fell over the room at his entrance and all eyes turned to him. And then Aunt Mimi gave a loud gasp, ran to him, and enfolded him in her arms.

"Look at you," she exclaimed as if his sudden arrival was nothing out of the ordinary. "How you've grown! But I would always recognize you. Your eyes and mouth are so like your mother's. Come, Lilly," she said turning, "come and see who has come to visit. You remember your cousin, don't you?" A silent, slender girl stepped forward from the shadows. Her eyes darted nervously around the room and she bit her bottom lip as she moved wraith-like toward them.

"Lilly is rather quiet these days," Aunt Mimi explained tenderly. "She's witnessed too many disturbing scenes around here to have much left to say about anything. Come," she wrapped an arm around Lilly's shoulder and beckoned Hendrik with a tilt of her head, "we'll have more privacy here." She led them past curious stares to a back corner and unceremoniously sat on the hard wooden floor as if it was the most natural thing to do, gently guiding Lilly down with her. A couple who had been standing nearby politely moved away as Hendrik joined his aunt and cousin on the floor.

Chapter 8

For the next half hour, Aunt Mimi quizzed him on the well-being of his mother and father. She wanted him to describe their apartment, to tell her about his school and his friends. They chatted as if his sudden visit here in this crowded apartment was the most ordinary thing in the world. But then suddenly she leaned forward and rubbed his arm up and down. "How healthy you are!" she whispered wistfully, as if to herself. "If only Gabor was here to see you. He is off as usual scavenging for whatever food scraps he can find for us. I guess your father did the right thing, to take you away when he could."

"That's why I came," Hendrik blurted out. "I missed you all. I came because I wanted to see you. I want to know why we can't see you anymore, why we left."

Aunt Mimi remained silent as Hendrik continued. "Father, he – he forbids me to talk about you. I can't ask him or Mother why we left without you." He looked down at his feet, ashamed of speaking about his parents like this. He was painfully aware of the tremor that had crept into his voice and worried that his words made no sense at all. "I just need to know," he added.

"I understand," Aunt Mimi finally responded, laying her hand lightly on his shoulder. "These are difficult times, and the wisest among us have difficulty figuring out what is going on or what to do. Your father did what he thought was best for you and your mother. He wanted to protect you, to keep you safe. He suspected from the beginning that the Jews of Hungary would not be spared in this war. Yes," she nodded to herself, "we were the foolish ones. Your Uncle Peter was too vocal about his political views, so they shipped him off to a forced labor camp. But your father was more careful. He saw what was coming and took action. Within weeks he had obtained false papers for all of you. He got himself a new job and a new home on the other side of the river.

"Most of these last five years I have been upset with your father because he separated our family. There seemed to be no reason for the drastic measures he had taken. We continued to live comfortably despite the restrictions we faced. I even kept hoping that your Uncle Peter would be allowed to come home. Even after the Nazis came, none of us thought it would become as bad here for the Jews as it was in other parts of Europe. That it would come to this." She gestured with her arm toward the room and the streets beyond the grimy window.

She leaned in close to him and whispered, "I've heard rumors that they line up hundreds of Jews daily by the Danube and shoot them into the river. Is it true? Have you seen it happen?"

Hendrik shook his head, horrified. *No. That could not be true.* Yet he recalled the group of Jews that the guards on Erzsebet Bridge had rounded up just before they accosted him. He remembered the shots that had rung out after him as he'd hurried away on his bicycle.

"Why couldn't you all come with us?" he asked. "Uncle Peter was already gone. Father left you here to fend for yourselves."

"I'm sure he would have helped us, too, if he could. But his money would only stretch so far. Your new life – it came at quite a price. He bought new identities for all of you. Your father's first responsibility was toward you and your mother." She shrugged. "As for us? He knew I was tough. And you see, we've survived. Your father did what he thought was best," she repeated. "He sacrificed a lot to start over."

Sacrifice? Hendrik pictured Father in his starched white shirts, expensive suits and silk ties in their spacious apartment. He thought of the lavish meals Magda and Mother prepared on weekends to entertain Father's business friends. Could they not have done with less? He looked around him and noted the crowded squalor of the room, how thin and frail Lilly was, the dark smudges under Aunt Mimi's eyes, their threadbare clothing.

And what about he himself? Hendrick squirmed uncomfortably on the wooden floor, suddenly ashamed of the muscles he had been so proud of, the collection of books that lined the shelves in his bedroom, his shiny new bicycle leaning against the ghetto wall. He saw Lilly shiver and quickly took off his sweater.

"Here," he said, awkwardly handing it to her, "take this. I don't need it. It – it's too stuffy in here." Before she could object, he turned back to Aunt Mimi.

"But why did Father forbid us to see you, to even talk about you? Or about anything in our past? I had to forget everything." The bitter injustice of the past five years washed over him and he felt the sting of tears in his eyes. Again Aunt Mimi shrugged.

"It was safer that way, I suppose," she answered. "He couldn't take a chance that one of you would say something to give away the truth in front of the wrong people or in the wrong place. He never even told me your new names or address. Perhaps he was scared that we would come calling." She laughed to herself at the ridiculousness of the thought. "The only person who could accompany your family was Magda. She was Catholic and had been in his service for most of her life. There was nothing for her to hide. I believe she was the one who set him up with the necessary contacts. I'm sure she was very helpful in teaching your parents all the Catholic customs they had to pretend to have known since childhood."

"But it wasn't right, what Father did," he argued. "If he couldn't bring you with us, we should have stayed. Our family should have stayed together."

Aunt Mimi squeezed his shoulder. "It's more complicated than that. Do you think you would be happier here with us, crammed into this room with not enough food to eat? No! Your father was the smart one. He made the right choice for you."

There it was. Her verdict. As if she knew the exact question he needed answered. But the answer wasn't that simple. He felt terribly sad for himself and for his family. Not knowing how to express what was in his heart, he remained silent and slowly pulled out the food he had salvaged from home. How meager his offering seemed. Yet it brought tears of appreciation to Aunt Mimi's eyes. In the distance a clock chimed. Three o'clock. Suddenly, Aunt Mimi was urging him toward the door.

Chapter 9

"You've got to leave now! The patrols often come mid-afternoon, searching the apartments," Aunt Mimi said in a concerned voice. "They want to account for everyone present. You mustn't be found here. You should have nothing to do with us."

Hendrik was defiant. "I belong here!" he countered. "I should never have left. I see that now. We are a family. We must support each other."

"Well, you won't be any good to us here," Aunt Mimi insisted while firmly guiding him toward the door. "Just another mouth to feed with food we don't have. If you leave, you can at least come back and bring more food."

"Yes," said Hendrik, somewhat hurt by her words, but still determined. "I will come back. Maybe tomorrow or the next day, with more supplies – I promise. I will make sure you don't starve. And when I return," he stopped and faced her, "maybe you can teach me about…"

"Yes, yes," she cut him off, clearly impatient as she nudged him on. Hendrik complied. When he came back, there would be time to learn all he wanted to know about their Jewish heritage. To learn the kinds of things Gabor must have learned when preparing for his bar mitzvah. Only then would Hendrick be able to choose as Brother Ferenc had suggested. And in return, he would become their champion. He would make sure they had everything they needed. Not only his family, but also the other people who were crowded into the room. He would also help all those poor distraught people he had seen in the streets. He would become the hero of the ghetto!

So absorbed was he in his fantasy that when he stepped through the front door of the building, he bumped right into the chest of an Arrow Cross soldier.

His gaze traveled up to the face of the uniformed man in front of him. Their eyes locked.

"Why, Hendrik," he heard a familiar voice say, "whatever are you doing here?"

It was Sergeant Biro, Ivan's father.

Hendrik couldn't think straight. His mind was too full of all that he had witnessed and heard in the past few hours. He was too full of plans to better the lives of his aunt and his cousins. His heart was too full of anger and regret over his absence from their lives during the past five years. He was too upset over the circumstances of the people he had seen in the ghetto – his people.

It was all the fault of people like Ivan's father. Sergeant Biro and others like him were responsible for the plight of his aunt and cousins. It was the soldiers of the Arrow Cross who were responsible for all the suffering he had witnessed on his short trip through the ghetto. Hendrik wanted to have nothing more to do with the Arrow Cross or with Sergeant Biro.

He raised his hands and pushed against Sergeant Biro's chest.

"I'm not Hendrik," he declared proudly. "I'm Jakob. Jakob Kohn. And I am a Jew."

Chapter 10

Someone's rough hands grabbed Jakob by the shoulders. A searing pain blinded him momentarily as he was slapped hard across the cheeks. Blood spurted from his nose.

"What do you mean by pushing an officer?" The soldier threw him to the ground and pointed a gun at his head. Behind him, Aunt Mimi screamed and Lilly started to cry.

"Wait!" Ivan's father ordered. Then he turned back to the boy. "What is this about, Hendrik? Or is it Jakob now? What are you saying? What kind of game of deception has your family been playing with us? With my Ivan?" Sergeant Biro leaned down and looked at him closely. Sudden understanding flared in his eyes, and his features altered. His friendly demeanor was now completely gone, replaced by anger. Slowly, Sergeant Biro straightened up. "Yes, yes. I see you are telling me the truth now," he said thoughtfully and shook his head. "You dared to lie to us. To me! To my son! You will suffer dearly for this!" With each sentence his voice rose, until he was shouting at Jakob.

"What else could we do but lie?" Jakob shouted back, his anger taking full control. "We had no choice. It's all the fault of people like you. Why are you doing this to us? Jews are just like everyone else. You know our family. You know me." Tears of frustration sprung to Jakob's eyes as he struggled to free himself from the iron grip of the soldiers.

"Take him away," Sergeant Biro commanded. "And arrest these people associated with him and take them too. I want to give our friend *Jakob* here a taste of what he has been missing all this time. He will learn not to deceive us again." He sneered as he spoke Jakob's name.

Before Jakob could protest, a young man rounded the corner. Jakob recognized the dark, thick line of his brows, the prominent cheekbones and full lips. Gabor! For an instant his heart lurched with hope. His older cousin Gabor had always come to his rescue in the past. He would know how to set things right.

"Mother! Lilly!" Gabor shouted, running up to them.

"Ah, another one," grinned Sergeant Biro. "Take him as well." There was no chance to explain anything. His aunt and Lilly were prodded at gunpoint to climb into the back of a nearby truck already crowded with Jews of all ages. Gabor, proud and defiant, resisted. Yanking his arm free from the soldier's grip, he reached out and grabbed the barrel of the gun pointed at his mother.

A shot exploded. With horror, Jakob watched Gabor's body crumple to the ground. Again Aunt Mimi screamed and lurched toward her son, but strong arms and guns barricaded her way, forcing her into the truck.

It was Jakob's turn to follow. In shock, he forced one foot in front of the other, desperate to avoid causing any more harm.

"Ivan!" Sergeant Biro's voice boomed above his head. Jakob saw his friend step forward from the shadows of the building. Ivan's face was white with shock. "Ivan," the Sergeant repeated, "I want you to hurry home and alert the patrols on our street. All of the Vargas, or whatever their name is, are to be rounded up at once. Their housekeeper included. Get one of the soldiers outside the gate to drive you. I can't spare any of my men here. We have more work to do."

Jakob stopped in mid-step. Ivan! Ivan was his friend. Thank goodness he was here! Ivan would insist that his father stop and release them. He would understand why Jakob hadn't said anything about his real identity before this. Surely Ivan would explain to his father that there were good reasons for Jakob's deception.

But Ivan didn't say a word. He opened his mouth but no words came out. He darted a quick glance from his father to Jakob, then back to his father. Then he pressed his lips together in a determined, straight line. From beneath his frowning brows, his eyes pierced a steely blue. He clenched his fists and remained silent, a shocked look on his face.

"Ivan!" Sergeant Biro's voice boomed again.

"Yes sir!" Ivan, straight and tall in his borrowed Arrow Cross uniform, saluted his father.

It was then, and only for an instant, that Ivan again glanced at Jakob. Their eyes met in recognition. He nodded his head almost imperceptibly at Jakob. The exchange between the boys had taken but a moment. Then Ivan turned on his heels and vanished from sight.

Jakob watched Ivan's retreating form. He saw Ivan break into a run. *He's going off to arrest the rest of my family, to betray us all. Ivan is no longer my friend, but my enemy. I will never forgive him,* Jakob vowed.

The gun prodded him again and Jakob stumbled onto the truck.

At almost every block in the ghetto, the truck stopped to collect more people, until no more could be squeezed in. Were they going to be shot by the river, as Aunt Mimi had described? And where in the truck were Aunt Mimi and Lilly? Unable to move around, he could not find them in the crowded space but thought that he could distinguish their anguished cries.

It was dusk when they finally reached their destination. Jakob recognized it immediately: the Eastern railway station of Budapest. It was the station he and Father had left from last summer on a fishing trip to a small lake in the mountains. He remembered his impatience to reach their destination, to sit in a boat, dangle his worm into the deep waters, and feel the tug of the giant fish he was certain of snagging. He remembered how he had hoped that since they would be alone, far from any curious ears, he could ask Father about the turn their lives had taken. But just as he had failed to catch the large fish, he had also failed to find the courage to broach the forbidden subject.

The prisoners were ordered off the truck and joined hundreds of others already waiting in strictly guarded lines. With both regret and relief, Jakob looked for his aunt and cousin, but could not find them. He couldn't bear to face them. They must despise him now for the calamity he had brought upon them.

A freight train arrived pulling a string of cattle cars. The doors to the cars were slid open and the people on the platform were shoved on. When anyone resisted, they were beaten or shot on the spot. Shot, just as Gabor had been shot.

When Jakob was forced into the cattle car, he discovered that it was already filled to capacity, yet more and more people were crowded in. All of them had the yellow Star of David stitched to their outer garments, identifying them as Jews. All except for Jakob.

Chapter 11

Jakob lost all track of time as he sat huddled in his corner of the over-crowded cattle car. His back and legs grew stiff. He was accidentally kicked and stepped on several times. Hunger gnawed at his insides.

He didn't care. He almost welcomed the pain and discomfort – a just punishment for his stupidity. He couldn't escape the horror of the day's events or his own self-reproach for what he had caused. His excuses of *I was only trying to help* and *I just wanted to stand up for Aunt Mimi and Lilly* seemed lame and childish now, even to him. He shook his head in an attempt to rid his mind of the painful thoughts and images. *I'm sorry. I didn't mean for any of this to happen. I am so sorry.* He repeated this litany over and over. He even mouthed the brief prayer Brother Ferenc had taught them to say before confessing their sins to a priest. Nothing brought him relief.

But recalling Brother Ferenc brought to mind something else

that the friar had taught them. "It is not enough to say that you are sorry," he would say to the boys. "If you are truly sorry for what you have done, you must also ask yourself the question, 'What can I do to make it right?'"

"Nothing," Jakob mumbled angrily to himself. What *could* he do? He couldn't bring Gabor back to life. He couldn't take back his reckless admission to Ivan's father that his family was Jewish. He couldn't force the guards to free his aunt and Lilly. He couldn't stop Ivan from leading the Arrow Cross soldiers to his parents and Magda. There was nothing he could do from this freight train that was taking him to an unknown destination.

Jakob only regained an awareness of his surroundings when a blast of cold air suddenly struck his face. The train had stopped. The freight car door was open. The sky outside was dark, except for a thin line of pale gray along the horizon. It would be dawn soon. Jakob realized that many hours had passed since they'd left the station in Budapest. Almost an entire day. A foul-smelling bucket, their toilet, was passed from hand to hand and dumped outside. Jakob aimed his nose at a small opening, a knothole in one of the planks near his face. He inhaled deeply of the crisp, fresh air.

After the bucket was emptied, the car door was slammed shut and the train rumbled on. They made many such stops along the way, sometimes for hours at a time. As they passed through fields, forests, and towns, Jakob observed the scene through his knothole, which served as a tiny window. At times he dozed, his head resting on his knees, warmed by the press of bodies around him.

It was in the misty, early dawn of the following day, when they stopped yet once more, that Jakob witnessed a horrific scene through his knothole. Two of the guards threw one body after another out onto the barren ground from the cars ahead of his. One was unmistakably that of a child. Other prisoners from the train were forced at gunpoint to walk a short distance, then shot. The guards left the bodies where they fell and returned to the train.

Shocked, Jakob looked at the men, women, and children around him. They were ignorant of what had just happened outside. He opened his mouth and reached forward to tug on the coattail of the woman closest to him. Suddenly his own car door opened and a soldier demanded if there were any people dead or ill in the car who needed attention. Several of the people in the car were elderly, some obviously sick. Unsuspecting, a few called out for assistance. Jakob wanted to shout out to them to remain quiet, but fear stopped him. What would the soldiers do to him if he yelled out a warning? There was some shuffling as those prisoners left the car, then the door clanged shut. He could hear the shots.

When the train stopped again they were finally ordered to dismount and line up. The sun was already low in the sky; Jakob's second full day on the train was nearing its end. Each prisoner was handed a small bowl of thin soup and a hunk of stale bread. A bucket of water was placed on the ground from which they could appease their thirst by scooping up mouthfuls with their hands. All too soon, Jakob finished his allotted portion, his stomach still craving more.

Once back on the train, Jakob paid closer attention to the conversations around him. There was much speculation about where they were heading and what awaited them. One person was convinced that they were being taken to a labor camp. Others hoped that they were simply being relocated to villages outside the border, where Jews were still tolerated. But some whispered about death camps where people were massacred by the thousands.

Life in a labor camp. That seemed the most likely possibility to Jakob. He might even be reunited with Uncle Peter. Jakob wasn't afraid of hard work. It would help him to stay in shape. And surely they would be better fed if they were expected to work hard. Perhaps he would find Aunt Mimi and Lilly and could be of help to them in some small way, filling the gap left by Gabor. He would take care of them. He would be given another opportunity to prove himself a man.

The train stopped again, jolting Jakob awake from a fitful, uncomfortable sleep. Through the knothole, he peered outside. The desolate landscape was bathed in sunlight. Another day had begun. There was a slight curve in the track ahead, which gave him a clear view of what was happening. The track was intersected in the middle by a narrow road with a large pickup truck parked across it, barring the train's progress. A couple of men in suits jumped down from the truck, each clutching a sheaf of papers. They hurried toward the guards who had dismounted from the train, and for a while it appeared to Jakob that the men argued – gesticulating with their arms toward the train, stabbing with their fingers at the papers, the guards shaking their heads.

Jakob could not hear what was being said outside. He couldn't even tell if the men from the truck were Arrow Cross or Nazis; they wore no uniforms. It was only because of their bearing, and the way the guards eventually seemed to succumb to them, that Jakob guessed they had some greater authority. One of the guards took the papers and, with the others following, turned toward the train. A few minutes later, Jakob watched as a small group of prisoners was herded away from the train, prodded roughly with gun barrels. Recalling that other early-morning scene, he knew without a doubt that they were being led to their deaths.

Through his peephole, about four car-lengths down, he saw a flash of green and orange among the people scurrying outside their car. His sweater! It must be Lilly. It was then with horror that Jakob looked more carefully. It *was* Lilly, without a doubt, embraced as always by her mother's protective arms.

Jakob's body went numb as he imagined the fate that awaited them. He cupped his hands over his ears so that he could not hear the gunshots. He squeezed his eyes shut, desperate to block out all sight and sound. He rocked back and forth for a long time as tears streamed down his cheeks.

He remained like that for a long time, oblivious to the jostling of bodies around him. He did not hear the screech of the door as it was slid open, the shouts of the guards as they repeatedly yelled into the car. He did not hear the clang as the door was slammed shut again. It was only when he felt the vibration of the train as it resumed its slow journey that he knew it was over. In his mind, he could see the bodies of Aunt Mimi and Lilly, left behind.

Chapter 12

Jakob slumped back into his corner in the car, consumed with guilt over the lives lost because of his thoughtless admission. What were his parents and Magda doing now? Were they too, on a train like this? Were they even still alive?

At least *their* fate wasn't his fault alone. Ivan was the one responsible for whatever was happening to them! Why hadn't Ivan stood by Jakob? Why hadn't he done something to stop his father? If he had said something in Jakob's defense, surely Sergeant Biro would have reconsidered their punishment.

How dare he just walk away, turning his back on Jakob without saying a word? Ivan had always been shrewd and good with words. Where was he now, when Jakob needed him? On their adventures, Ivan had always known what to do and say to get them out of trouble. But this time he'd said nothing. *Just because he discovered that I am Jewish.*

Jakob recalled again that piercing look in Ivan's eyes, his clenched fists. That strange little nod before he walked away. And then he imagined Ivan with the Arrow Cross soldiers going back to his home to capture his parents and Magda. If Ivan had acted differently, perhaps none of this would have happened. Jakob wouldn't be on this horrible train. Aunt Mimi and Lilly would still be alive. Jakob's parents and Magda would still be safe at home.

No. All this wasn't Jakob's fault at all. It was Ivan's. *He's the one who should be suffering.* In frustration, Jakob rammed his knuckles into the side of the boxcar. *I'll get him back for this,* he vowed. *Somehow I will get back home to find him. No matter what lies ahead, I'll return and make Ivan pay.* With the passing of each kilometer, Jakob's resolve strengthened, distracting him from his own pain and from all that he had recently witnessed.

After what seemed like an eternity of hunger, stiff limbs, and suffocating air, the doors slid open. Jakob was greeted by double rows of barbed-wire fencing and a multitude of Nazi soldiers who surrounded the train, yelling one command after another in German. The orders sounded menacing. The presence of clubs, guns, and the vicious guard dogs that prowled among the officers added weight to their urgency.

"Stay with me," Jakob whispered to the ghost of Ivan. "With your help, I will return to Budapest and repay you for what you have done! It will be my life's mission to seek revenge."

People dismounted, squinting in the bright daylight, hugging their outer garments close to their bodies. Jakob had only his thin shirt. The fresh breeze from the open doorway chilled the drops of sweat on his back. A moment ago he had been sweltering among a mass of bodies. Now he shivered as he stepped out onto the platform. They had arrived at their destination: Auschwitz.

67

The train took Jakob and the other Jews from Budapest to Auschwitz in Poland.

PART TWO

Jakob and hundreds of other Jews were taken out of the cattle cars and ordered to assemble on the ramp at Auschwitz-Birkenau concentration camp.

Chapter 13

November 9, 1944

When they first disembarked from the train, hundreds of exhausted men, women, and children were separated amid a barrage of yelling and wailing. Families were brutally split apart and only infants were allowed to remain with their mothers. Women and children were shoved to the left, men and boys to the right.

Jakob scanned the windswept yard, looking for any means of escape. The whole area was bordered by double rows of barbed-wire fencing that stretched as far as the eye could see. It was swarming with guards with drawn bayonets at the ready, some with vicious-looking dogs at their side. Wooden watchtowers loomed in the distance. Behind the train stood a long stone building with an open arch through which the tracks disappeared – the only possible route back toward freedom and home. *What would Ivan do if he were here?*

Once the Jews were lined up, they
went through a selection process.
Jakob knew he had to look strong
in order to stay alive. The sick and
elderly were separated and were
sent to their deaths.

Jakob wondered. *What sort of scheme would Ivan come up with to get them out of here? Pay attention to what's going on,* he imagined Ivan's voice prompting him. *It might make a difference which group you are in.* It was the same advice Ivan had always given when they had lined up for various sports teams or school assignments.

Jakob, weary from lack of food and sleep, forced himself to observe the sorting process more closely. He stood amid a throng of men and boys. One by one, they were made to approach a table where a seated guard barked a few simple questions at them. Depending on the answers given, they were directed to go to the left or the right. Jakob noticed that the left contained very young boys and sickly or elderly men. To the right were the healthy, young, more muscular men and a few adolescents – none, by the looks of them, younger than fifteen or sixteen. *Left, death. Right, life.* Jakob nodded his acknowledgement, not caring if the voice in his head was a mere delusion. He wasn't sure what awaited either group, but clearly there was more hope for the one on the right. As he moved closer to the table and the seated guard, he squared his shoulders and flexed his muscles. He knew his survival was at stake.

"Name!" boomed the guard.

"Jakob Kohn." He hoped his voice sounded sufficiently deep.

"Place of birth."

"Budapest."

"Age."

Jakob hesitated for only an instant. "Sixteen." The guard looked up, scrutinized him for a long moment. Then he nodded to the right. "Next," he bellowed.

Jakob stood with this ever-expanding group for a very long time. There were only three other boys that looked like they too might have lied about their age. They exchanged weak, relieved smiles, but were too frightened to speak. Every once in a while, a shot rang out. This was a signal to all that someone among the prisoners had been shot for disobeying. Jakob knew that no matter what happened he must not do anything to draw attention to himself. He must do nothing that might entice one of the guards to shoot him on the spot.

After hours of standing, when even the strongest among them looked like they might collapse, they were given water and bread and allowed to sit on the cold, hard ground. Their respite lasted only a few minutes. Jakob had barely swallowed his last crumb when they were ordered to move.

Their group of "men" were marched for several kilometers down a road lined on either side with rows of long, low makeshift buildings: the barracks. The terrain was flat, the ground barren, though the odd tree, with its dying brown and yellow leaves, poked its crown above some of the buildings. A flock of wild ducks flew overhead, quacking loudly as if boasting of their freedom to fly wherever they wished. On the ground, men clothed in striped uniforms stood or sat outside the barracks and gazed listlessly at the marching prisoners. Jakob was shocked at how thin and emaciated they looked. How could they possibly do any hard labor in that state? Jakob wondered whether this was one of the labor camps he had heard about.

Eventually they arrived at a relatively small, square building where they were stripped of their clothing, shaved bald, and forced to shower. They were then tattooed on their arms with identification numbers. By the time he was handed a striped uniform made of coarse cotton and a pair of ill-fitting wooden clogs, Jakob no longer cared about his confiscated clothes, or how he would withstand the cold. He was too overwhelmed by the indignities he had been made to endure, too tired and famished to worry about anything but sleep and food.

He placed his right hand gingerly over his throbbing left arm. The number 18036 had been burned into his flesh. A searing pain scorched his heart more than his skin. This number would be his new identity.

Barbed wire fences enclosed
the entire camp.

Chapter 14

Each side of Jakob's barrack was lined with eighteen tiers of wooden beds, each tier three beds high with a thin mattress of straw on each. A long horizontal pipe ran down the length of the barrack along the floor. Jakob was to learn later that this was the "chimney" – or "stove," as some called it – which provided the only source of heat. The men only had a short while to contemplate their new living quarters. Within minutes, groups of prisoners with their guards arrived back at the yard and a roll call was taken.

Jakob soon learned to despise the roll calls, which took place before dawn each morning, at the end of every day, and on most days several times in between. Roll calls required the prisoners to stand – sometimes for hours at a time – in the barren, wind-swept yard between the barracks, regardless of the weather. SS guards and their Jewish underlings, the Kapos, made sure that all the prisoners remained standing at attention or, on occasion, squatting, or maybe even on their knees on the hard gravel surface – whatever the ones in charge happened to fancy. If prisoners did not obey, they were beaten with rubber clubs or rifles.

That first day, the Kapo guard in charge of their barrack strutted back and forth in front of the new arrivals. He repeatedly slapped his truncheon into the palm of his hand as he called out one number after another in German. Jakob struggled to understand the foreign words. Though he had learned some German at school, he was not fluent enough to comprehend the rapid drill of numbers fired at him now. His nervousness didn't help. Despite the cold, beads of sweat broke out on his forehead. His mounting fear confused him even more.

When someone failed to respond, the Kapo bulldozed his way through the rows of prisoners, yanking at arms, scrutinizing each man until he found the culprit. Blows to the culprit followed. Jakob's lips trembled and his eyes filled with tears of frustration. He could name his numbers individually in German, and slowly, but didn't know how to put them together. He almost missed the slight nudge on his left side. He looked up into the face of an older boy, or maybe he was a young man, who gave a meaningful glance toward the exposed number on Jakob's arm. Taking the cue, Jakob shouted the required "here." Relief flooded over him when the Kapo yelled out the next number.

This was the bleak landscape
that greeted the prisoners at
Auschwitz – row upon row of
cold wooden barracks.

Inside each barrack were banks of hard wooden sleeping platforms, three tiers high. Jakob had to share one platform, meant for two, with four other men.

For now, he had avoided a beating! He gave a guarded smile of appreciation to the boy on his left. Equally important to knowing one's number, as Jakob had quickly discovered, was the rule of silence among the prisoners during roll call.

When it was finally over, the Kapo regarded the forlorn, shivering group with a malevolent glint in his eyes. "Welcome to Auschwitz Concentration Camp!" he shouted in an icy tone that made Jakob tremble more than the frigid air around him did. "I'm Kapo Szekeres from Camp C-8 and you had best obey me."

Back in the barrack after roll call, Jakob learned from the other men that all Kapos were Jews. They had been picked from among the inmates to be in charge of the prisoners in the barracks. It had at first shocked Jakob to discover that Szekeres, the Kapo who treated them so brutally, was himself a prisoner. He had been chosen for the role of Kapo because of his violent reputation. Szekeres had his own private room at the front of the barrack. As long as he pleased their SS superiors and did their bidding, he was well fed and rarely disciplined. Even after just one day, Jakob could understand how someone might do anything to ensure himself a full stomach and a soft bed in this environment of hunger, cold, and hard labor.

Despite his fatigue, Jakob found it difficult to fall asleep that night. His bed was hard, and he felt cramped with two other men squeezed in next to him. He found himself silently mouthing the "Ave Maria," the prayer all the boys at the Catholic school had learned to recite daily. It was the prayer he habitually repeated at night whenever he had difficulty sleeping. It worked better than counting sheep. But the words failed to have their hypnotic effect as he struggled to keep disturbing thoughts and memories at bay. In vain he tried to remember some of the Hebrew prayers he used to know as a small child. The only words that came to him were *Barukh atah adonai*, then he drew a blank. He sighed. He didn't even know what those Hebrew words meant. So much for the Jewish heritage that he had so foolishly tried to defend.

When he had made the decision to seek out his aunt and cousins, Jakob had assumed that he would be able to learn about Judaism from Gabor. After all, Gabor had already had his bar mitzvah – the ceremony marking a Jewish boy's transition to manhood. "After my bar mitzvah I will be responsible for my own actions and for following our faith – for keeping the traditions and upholding our law," a young Gabor had explained to an even younger Jakob. The similarity of those words to the ones later spoken by Brother Ferenc had struck Jakob.

All Jakob could remember of his cousin's bar mitzvah preparation were those words, and the fact that Gabor had attended Jewish classes on Saturday mornings. Their families hadn't been very religious. Not like some of the people living in their old neighborhood who walked to the synagogue every Saturday morning – the women in their wigs, the men in their black hats. Still, Mother and Aunt Mimi had lit the Sabbath candles every Friday night. They had celebrated Rosh

Hashanah, the Jewish new year, with a special dinner and fasted on Yom Kippur, the day of atonement. And the whole family would gather together for the seder meal on Passover.

Jakob regretted that he remembered so little of that time, of the Jewish traditions that had been part of his life when he was a young boy. Now he would never have the chance to ask Gabor about all that his cousin had learned for his bar mitzvah. If his whole family was destroyed, from whom would he learn about his Jewish heritage?

Chapter 15

Jakob soon discovered that the name of the tall, lanky boy who had saved him from a beating during that first roll call was Aron. But it wasn't until three days after Jakob arrived that he found the courage to thank him. Jakob was on his way to the latrine when he almost collided with Aron, who was smoking behind the barrack. While Jakob found that most of the men looked similar with their gaunt bodies and hollow cheeks, it was impossible to mistake Aron with the dense red fuzz of hair that covered his head within hours of being shaved.

Jakob was tempted to hurry past and pretend that he hadn't seen the forbidden activity. He imagined Ivan's voice coaxing him: *You need a friend. Here's your chance. Talk to him.* Jakob slowed his steps and forced himself to stop.

"How'd you manage to get that cigarette butt?" Jakob asked, trying to sound casual.

"I have friends in the right places," winked Aron. It was true. Jakob had observed that the man ladling the soup had slipped Aron an extra crust of bread the other day. He also had noticed the thicker blanket on Aron's bed, the woolen sweater he wore beneath his prisoner's uniform. Those were the necessities of survival, the kinds of things everyone tried their best to obtain. Cigarettes, on the other hand, were a rare luxury among the inmates. Having cigarettes was also punishable by a beating – something most of them tried to avoid.

Aron started to turn away from Jakob as if dismissing him, then seemed to change his mind. "Want a puff?" he asked.

"Sure! Thanks," said Jakob and reached for the stub even though he had never smoked a cigarette before. "And thank you for saving my neck the other day during roll call," he added before his courage failed him.

Too nervous to say anything else, he inhaled deeply on the cigarette and immediately collapsed into a fit of coughing. It was several minutes before he regained his composure, his eyes still watering from the harsh, bitter fumes. He was mortified by his obvious inexperience.

"First time, eh? Why didn't you say so? What's your name?" asked Aron good-naturedly.

"I'm Jakob," he replied.

"Here, have another, but take it slow and easy. Don't let it reach your lungs." Jakob tried again, successful this time. He handed the stub back to Aron, who scrutinized him from head to toe. "You're not sixteen yet, are you?" he asked. "Don't worry, your secret is safe with me. We all lie about something or other in order to survive. What's important is that set of muscles you have. Good workers don't get killed as long as they're careful. I bet you could even take on our Kapo without a problem. Not that I recommend you try. Though I'd like to see that filthy traitor get what he deserves." They both chuckled as they envisioned the Kapo lying bruised and bloody on the ground with Jakob standing proudly over him.

Emboldened by Aron's comment and recalling a boxing match he had read about, Jakob started to relay a mock play-by-play account of the imagined fight, inserting himself into the story, just as Hendrik had always done for Ivan.

"Today, young Jakob Kohn, the new lightweight recruit from Budapest, faces off with Kapo Szekeres of Camp C-8. The two opponents face each other. They circle. Szekeres punches the air beside Kohn's head several times. Kohn ducks. He delivers the first blow to the Kapo's soft belly. Szekeres doubles over in pain." As Jakob continued, Aron covered his mouth to stifle his laughter, wary of possibly attracting the notice of a nearby guard.

"Well done!" Aron slapped Jakob on the back. "That's a valuable talent you have. We don't get much entertainment around here." He pulled another butt from his pocket and lit it from the first. "But we shouldn't be too hard on our Kapo. He told me once that his wife and young son are prisoners here in Auschwitz as well. She works in the kitchen for the SS. The deal is that as long as the Kapo performs his duties well by SS standards, his family will stay unharmed. That's why he is especially harsh with us whenever there are any SS guards overseeing roll call."

"Which seems to be most of the time," said Jakob. Aron nodded and passed the butt.

"So how'd you come by these?" Jakob asked again as he lifted the cigarette to his lips.

"Antol, the Jew who cleans the trash in the SS officers building, is from my hometown. I gave him my dinner ration one night when I noticed he was feverish and coughing. He's been repaying me ever since by pilfering valuables like these from the garbage for me."

"That was very noble of you, to give your dinner away like that," said Jakob with obvious admiration. It was difficult to imagine forgoing even a fraction of their meager meals.

"Oh, there was nothing all that noble about it," smirked Aron. "We all do whatever it takes to survive. I knew what I was doing. I knew Antol was assigned to the SS building and that it could only benefit me to be kind to him. Giving him that meal was the best investment I've made since being here. Since then, I've bartered stubs, pages from magazines, any Nazi trash that Antol swipes – for other necessities."

Jakob contemplated the cigarette end between his fingers.

"This smoke, then, is an 'investment' in me?" he asked.

"A butt for a story? Right now I can't imagine a better investment than that," winked Aron. "I hope you'll tell me more in the future."

"You seem to know the rules of survival here very well," said Jakob. "Have you been here long?"

"No one is here for long, and no one escapes," said Aron with a smirk. "The whole point of Auschwitz as far as I can see is to kill us off as quickly as possible – whether it's through starvation, hard labor, beatings, or the gas chambers."

"Gas chambers?" asked Jakob. The lack of food, the beatings, and the exhausting, heavy work he had already witnessed, but gas chambers?

"What do you think those smokestacks are for?" Aron nodded toward a series of tall brick chimneys in the distance. "What do you think causes that putrid stench that greets us whenever the wind blows in this direction?" Jakob shuddered.

"So how long have you been here?" he asked again, wanting to change the subject.

"In Auschwitz?" Aron paused for a minute, calculating. "I know it's the twelfth of November today because I've got a calendar tacked to the bottom of the bunk above mine. I don't want to lose track of time. I arrived at the beginning of July, so I would say about four months. But," he added, hunching his shoulders forward as if trying to fold into himself, "I've been away from home for longer than that. My real home, that is. I'm from Debrecen. In the middle of May, my mother, two sisters, and I were forced to move to the ghetto. Thousands of us were cramped into a small area," Aron shook his head as if lacking the words to explain. "It was horrible," he said simply.

"I know," nodded Jakob. "I've seen the one in Budapest."

"We thought it had been bad before, with one law after another being passed limiting our lives as Jews. A month later, we were put on separate trains and I ended up here. I have no idea where my mother and sisters are."

"What about your father? You haven't mentioned him. What happened to him?"

"He was drafted into forced labor in 1939. As far as we know he ended up in the Ukraine. We never heard from him again," Aron sighed and threw away his burned-out stub.

"That's about the time when my uncle was drafted too. Maybe they're together," said Jakob. The two boys shared a smile for a moment as they imagined the two men talking, making friends just as they were. Jakob could almost feel Ivan patting him on the back: *Well done. You won't be needing me anymore.*

But, as the days progressed, Jakob found that he did still need Ivan – though not for friendship. Ivan always figured in his thoughts. During the hardest times at the camp, Jakob would focus his anger on Ivan. The thought of getting back at Ivan kept Jakob's blood circulating through his veins. He was determined to return to Budapest and seek his revenge. This is what kept him alive.

Chapter 16

Jakob might have lost all sense of time had it not been for Aron's calendar marking the tedious passage of days. Each was the same as the last, except that the days grew steadily colder as autumn crept into winter. One morning, he could see his breath as it escaped through his chattering teeth. A few mornings later, a thin layer of frost covered the dull gray gravel between the barracks.

The men were roused early, well before dawn, and assembled for roll call. They shivered in their thin uniforms, anxious to go to work, welcoming any diversion from the bone-numbing chill of immobility. After a breakfast of weak tea and stale bread, they were marched off to their various designated jobs. The yelling and cursing of the guards, the beatings, even the deaths soon became as commonplace to Jakob as his bleak surroundings.

When they returned at the end of each day, Jakob would scan the group, looking for the red stubble of Aron's head. When their eyes connected, their lips would twitch with a barely perceptible smile. They had survived another day!

Jakob knew that there was an unspoken understanding among the prisoners that friendships were not to be formed. Too many people died each day. They all suffered enough without the added anguish of losing someone they cared for. Besides, it seemed that almost every country in Europe was represented in Auschwitz, even in Jakob's barrack. A multitude of languages were spoken by the inmates but few were understood by everyone. Most of the men kept to themselves, only communicating with each other when necessary. The one language they all soon learned was German, as barked at them by the SS guards.

The number of men grew steadily as herds of fresh prisoners arrived daily. It was the second last day of November when another bedraggled group of new prisoners marched past while they were outside for roll call. Jakob sighed. More arrivals meant less space in his already cramped bed, which he now shared with three others. It meant longer lines for the latrines, and possibly even more meager rations. The new arrivals, despite the miserable conditions they had likely endured during their transport to Auschwitz, still looked fresh and well fed in comparison with the hollow-cheeked skeletons surrounding Jakob in the yard.

As the new prisoners slowly filed past, one head of dark curls stood out among the rest. It belonged to a tall young man with a proud bearing who, instead of dragging his feet like the others, walked with a determined, brisk step. A twisted strand of long hair dangled down either side of his face and he twirled one of these round and round between his right thumb and index finger – the only sign of the agitation from beneath his otherwise composed exterior. He had a short beard and wore a small skull cap balanced precariously on the back of his head. *He must be an Orthodox Jew from one of those close-knit rural Jewish communities*, thought Jakob.

He exchanged a look with Aron, who stood next to him. "I bet he won't last long," Aron whispered out of the corner of his mouth. "He looks pretty useless. He's probably more accustomed to studying the Talmud than exerting himself physically. The Nazis will finish him off in no time." Jakob's eyes darted nervously toward the Kapo. Aron's daring whisper could easily bring down a torrent of heavy blows upon his back. But the Kapo was distracted by the creeping column of men coming toward them.

At the end of the long, tiring day of hauling rocks, Jakob dragged himself through the barrack doors. When he looked toward his allotted bed space, his heart sank. One of the new prisoners, with freshly shorn head and striped uniform, stood there. Jakob sighed. Now there would be five men sleeping on the hard wooden boards originally built for two.

"Hello, I'm Levi," the young man extended his hand to shake

Jakob's. "I was told to share – this," he hesitated for a moment, as if uncertain what to call the barren planks. "This bed," he said at last with a resigned shrug. Without looking at him, Jakob mumbled his own name in response and ignored the outstretched hand, too concerned that sleep, almost as scarce as food, would now be even more difficult to come by.

It was only later, during yet another roll call, when he noticed his new bed mate nervously rubbing his fingers together near his cheek, that Jakob realized Levi was the man who had arrived with the side locks of hair. Now, with his head and beard shaved, he looked no older than Aron. Jakob felt a sudden pang of guilt for his earlier rudeness and almost blurted out an apology on the spot. What was the point? It wasn't worth risking a beating.

Later that night, as the prisoners crawled wearily into bed, Levi remained standing at the side of theirs, his eyes closed, gently rocking back and forth on his feet and whispering unintelligible words. "What are you doing?" Jakob hissed. "You'll get a beating if you don't get in promptly."

Levi opened his eyes. "It is the beginning of the Sabbath tonight. It is already past the time for prayers, but I think God will understand."

"Sabbath!" the man on Jakob's other side sneered. "There is no Sabbath, no day of rest here."

"*Sabbath* is in my heart. I can always rest with God there. No one can stop that," Levi said and returned to his prayers. Strangely,

94

the Kapo did not notice the lone figure that remained standing in the shadows.

It was only later, when Levi climbed in next to him, that Jakob realized Aron had been wrong. Levi *was* of some use. He occupied the outmost edge of the bed, the spot that had previously belonged to Jakob. This way, as Jakob lay on his side, Levi's long, solid frame, pressed by necessity close to his, shielded and warmed him. For the first time since he had arrived, Jakob slept without disruption from the biting cold against his back.

Chapter 17

It was Jakob's advice that Levi sought whenever he needed to know some detail about the workings of the camp. Maybe it was because they shared a bunk, or maybe because Jakob was younger and therefore more approachable. At first, it embarrassed Jakob to be asked for advice by someone older than he was. But gradually he became more comfortable with Levi and started asking his own questions.

"What language are you using? Why are you praying? What do your prayers mean? "

"I pray in Hebrew," Levi had responded, sounding surprised at Jakob's question. "It's the language we all use for prayers. *Barukh atah adonai, eloheinu melekh ha'olam.* Those are the words that most of our prayers start with: 'Blessed are you, Lord, our God, sovereign of the universe.'"

"Though I am a Jew, I was never taught to pray like that," Jakob replied. "At least, not that I remember. My parents, they – for years now – they pretended we were Catholic. I went to a Catholic school. They thought it would protect us." The shame Jakob had felt when he visited Aunt Mimi in the ghetto washed over him again.

Levi nodded in sympathy. "I'm sure God understands. Your parents did what they thought was best," he said softly. "I know that many Jews who had the means bought false identities. Besides," he smiled, "it's not that easy to truly get rid of your Jewish identity. You were born a Jew and no paper document can change what is in your blood. Even in my town of Mako, where there were many Orthodox Jews, I think some would have considered fleeing had they suspected what was coming. My father was a teacher at the *cheder*, the Jewish religious school for young boys. In our town, we all knew each other, Jews and Christians alike. We all lived together comfortably. Our town was totally unprepared for the Nazi soldiers when they stormed in with their guns and bayonets to round up all the Jews. Of course we all knew what had taken place in other countries, but we never thought it would spread to Hungary. Especially not to our town of Mako." Levi looked down at his hands clasped in his lap.

"I was delivering some of my mother's fresh, sweet rolls to a Christian neighbor. We had heard that their son was not well and Mother wanted to cheer him up. I was talking with his mother at the door when the Nazis stormed into town. She immediately ordered me to go down into the root cellar. I was very frightened." Levi paused, pressed his lips tight, and raised a hand to rub his fingers around his now-absent lock of hair. "I was torn between running out to join my parents and younger sisters and hiding in my neighbor's cellar. But she was very insistent, and I did as she said. She hid me behind bags of onions and potatoes in a corner of the cellar. I later learned that the entire Jewish community was forced to move to a ghetto. From there they were moved to another town called Szeged and eventually brought to Auschwitz."

"But you are here now too," said Jakob. "What happened?"

"I lived in the cellar for several months before word leaked out that a Jew was in hiding there. The Arrow Cross arrived one day and arrested me and the whole family. Even the small children. I don't know where they were taken…" Levi's voice trailed off.

Jakob didn't know what to say. It was hard to comprehend how much everyone in this camp had already suffered.

"Now that I am here in Auschwitz myself, I keep looking for my family and for the Christian family who put their lives at risk for my sake. There are so many prisoners here, and so far I haven't found anyone I know."

For a few moments the boys sat silently, both contemplating the possible fate that might have befallen their loved ones.

Finally Levi changed the subject. "You were asking me about my prayers. It is Jewish religious custom to pray at least twice a day. In the morning, we thank God for waking us and we ask his help to do our work well. At night, we thank God for the work we did and ask for his blessing. We always thank him for all the good things he provides us." He sighed heavily. "Here it's difficult to say the prayers at the appropriate times, and they've taken away my skull cap and prayer shawl. But I trust God will understand that too."

"What can you possibly find to thank God for here in Auschwitz?" Jakob asked.

"I still have my life," Levi answered. "I have hope that my family still lives and that one day we will all be together again. I have you as a friend," Levi smiled. "I know it's difficult here – very difficult." He shook his head. "But I can't let that separate me from God. I wouldn't be much of a man if, just because I suffer, I forget God."

Chapter 18

Over the next few days, in the darkness of the night and in hushed tones, Jakob told Levi about his life as a Catholic and the mission that had sent him to the ghetto.

"You were fortunate to have a teacher like Brother Ferenc," said Levi. "He seems like a wise man, not afraid to face the truth or to give people the freedom to discover it for themselves. But if you really want to know which faith you would choose for yourself, you will need to learn about the religion you were born into. You should learn as much about the Jewish faith as you know about the Catholic one."

"Yes, I had hoped that there would be time for my aunt and cousin to teach me – but now they are gone," Jakob said, his eyes filling with tears.

As Jakob lay there, a new thought began to take shape in his mind. Perhaps he could learn all that he had missed out on over the years from Levi. He hungered for more knowledge about Judaism almost as much as his body hungered for food. And here was knowledgeable Levi beside him. He shifted on the hard boards trying to make out the contours of Levi's face.

"Can *you* teach me everything you know about the Jewish religion?" Jakob asked. Despite the dark he could sense the smile in Levi's response.

"I can try. But there is more to religion than memorizing prayers and learning traditions," Levi replied. "Jewish values, such as justice, honor, and helping others, are just as important a part of our religion. We should try to make the world a better place through our individual actions."

"As if there's any chance of us doing that here," Jakob scoffed.

"There are always opportunities to do good," Levi explained. "Even here."

And so Jakob's instruction began. As he learned the Hebrew words and their meanings, Jewish prayers slowly replaced the Christian ones that he had been taught. Each night before he closed his eyes, he tried to think of one good thing to be thankful for. *I didn't get beaten today. My slice of bread had no mold today.* Or sometimes he would remind himself, simply, as Levi had suggested, *I am still alive.*

Whenever they had a chance to be alone, Jakob and Levi engaged in animated discussions about the meaning and significance of Jewish values and Hebrew words.

"*Tzedakah* is much like Christian charity," explained Levi on one occasion. "Only in Judaism, it is our obligation to give to the poor and needy."

"Yes," Jakob nodded, recognizing not the word but the concept. "Brother Ferenc always said that even if we had no money to put in the collection plate that was passed around at mass, we could still give of ourselves. We could give of our time each week by visiting a sick person or helping out the elderly."

"Exactly," smiled Levi. "Even here in this prison camp we can try to help those who are suffering more than we are. We can show love and support to each other."

"You guys are wasting your time," Aron taunted more than once. "God, if there is one, has clearly forgotten about us. Spare your energies for surviving. For getting out of here alive."

But Jakob found that his discussions with Levi gave him much-needed support. Memorizing Hebrew prayers and contemplating Jewish customs and ideas had become part of his reason to stay alive. They transported him to a space beyond the gnawing cold, his hunger, and the painful sores on his hands and feet from the rough work he was forced to do. While hoisting rocks all day, he imagined Levi and Brother Ferenc sitting together with him in a comfortable living room and discussing the nature of love, charity, and justice. He now had another reason to live – beyond revenge.

Chapter 19

Thump! Thump! Thump! The slap of the baton against the Kapo's palm echoed in the misty dawn. He paced back and forth in front of the prisoners, who had been standing at attention for more than an hour.

"Let's play our little game," he said. "A reward for your good behavior."

Jakob's senses suddenly came alive. The game! The very thought made his mouth water. It was early, but never too early for a treat. Maybe this would be his lucky day and he would be picked. The other men, too, stared at the Kapo in eager anticipation. All except Levi.

The Kapo scanned the prisoners' faces, clearly relishing the power he had over them. His eyes settled on a frail middle-aged man. "Number 638," the Kapo yelled the last three digits of the prisoner's tattooed number as he hurled his baton a short distance down the field. "Fetch!"

Immediately, the weakened prisoner dropped to all fours and scurried after the club. Jakob bit his lips together to keep himself from laughing out loud at the ridiculous sight of the man as he wiggled and tottered from side to side, trying not to stumble on his loose pant legs. When he got to the baton, he gingerly picked it up with his teeth and hurried back in the same fashion, dropping the club at the Kapo's feet. Then, in keeping with the rules of the game, he sat back on his haunches and with arms bent in front, tongue hanging, panted and begged like a dog.

With great ceremony, the Kapo reached into his jacket pocket and pulled out a small candy wrapped in shiny cellophane. Carefully he freed the candy and tossed it into the air. Prisoner number 638 tilted up his head and followed its flight with his eyes. As the candy arched toward him, he opened his mouth wide. In an instant the candy disappeared from sight.

Jakob swallowed hungrily as he imagined the sweet treat melting in his own mouth. Then he sighed. Perhaps next time.

He avoided meeting Levi's eye as they trudged back to get in line for breakfast. They had argued about the game after the first time Levi had witnessed it. "It's totally humiliating," Levi had said with disgust. "And what makes it worse is that the Kapo himself is a Jew. He should know better than to treat his own people like dogs."

"The SS rewarded him lavishly for inventing the game," Aron replied. "I'm sure he gets extra rations whenever one of the SS sees him playing it. Have you noticed how he picks the occasions to dole out candy to coincide with one of the SS patrols passing by? Look at him," Aron sneered. "He's clearly not starving like the rest of us. Anyway, why should we forego a treat, no matter how we come by it? There's no other way you're going to be given sweets in this place."

Jakob had to agree. Though he too, had been shocked the first time he'd witnessed the humiliating game, after a few weeks of near starvation, he was as eager as the others to be picked.

"Well, you won't catch me scampering about like a dog," Levi said. "No matter what the reward."

As it turned out, Levi had nothing to worry about. Assuming that Levi, like the others, was eager to participate in his game, the Kapo never selected him. The Kapo seemed to have taken an intense dislike of Levi and often mocked his daily prayers. He singled out and punished Levi for the slightest transgressions. Once, he even gave Levi a lashing for sneezing during an imposed period of silence.

Chapter 20

"What's wrong?" Jakob asked Levi on a frosty December morning almost two weeks after Levi's arrival. It was, he knew, a ridiculous question. Everything was wrong. They were shivering, starving, and aching all over from their hard labor. They didn't even know if they would still be alive at the end of each day.

On this morning, Levi was unusually quiet. It was not the peaceful quiet that usually enveloped him after his morning prayer. No, this quiet was distracted and agitated.

"Tonight is the first night of Hanukkah and we have no candles to light."

"Hanukkah?" asked Aron, who had walked up beside them. "You're worried about not celebrating Hanukkah? We have bigger worries here, like staying alive." He waved his arm around the barrack, pointing to the assortment of emaciated and ailing prisoners. "We don't have the luxury of celebrating traditions here."

"But our Jewish traditions and history are important," insisted Levi. "They remind us of who we are as a people. Where we've come from. What God has done for us in the past and what he expects of us in the future. In difficult times like these, especially, it is good to remember the victory of the Maccabees and the miracle of the lights."

"It will be a miracle for us if we can manage to stay alive," said Aron. "That is all I would recommend you try to do."

"Staying alive with our bodies isn't enough. Not if who we are inside dies in the process," said Levi.

"Missing a few traditions shouldn't destroy our identity," said Aron.

"No, but observing them would certainly help in preserving who we are. It would help all of us."

"So what would you need?" asked Jakob, wanting to put an end to their bickering.

"A candle," said Levi, responding instantly. "Traditionally, it's nine candles – one for each of the eight nights of Hanukkah, plus one to light the other eight. A menorah to hold the candles. And a match. Some special food, like potato latkes, would be nice," he added, smiling mischievously at Aron. "It is a celebration after all."

"Why so many candles?" asked Jakob hurriedly. Their time was running out. Any minute now, the dreaded order to line up for roll call would put an end to all conversation.

"Hanukkah is two celebrations in one. The first commemorates the rebuilding and rededication of the temple after the victory of the Maccabees against their much stronger enemy. The word "Hanukkah" means rededication. The second reminds us about a miracle – the miracle of the lights. After rebuilding the temple many centuries ago, for its rededication to God, our ancestors needed a light to burn every night in the temple. This light is never allowed to go out, to show that God is always present. But the Jews only had enough sacred oil for one night. Yet, miraculously, the oil lasted for eight days. Since then, we remember the miracle by lighting candles for eight nights."

As Levi talked, an old memory surfaced in Jakob's mind. He remembered his family gathered around a menorah with eight curved branches, the flames casting beautiful flickering shadows across their faces as they blended their voices together in song. He remembered the smell of deep-fried food, the taste of the sweet applesauce on his tongue. He, Gabor, and Lilly playing with a wooden dreidel on the floor while their mothers fried latkes, potato pancakes, in the kitchen. He remembered the dining room, the parquet floor with its thick Persian carpet, the white tablecloth on the table, the glow from the menorah. Father handing out Hanukkah *gelt*, chocolate coins wrapped in gold foil, to the children after dinner. Most of all, he remembered the joy and laughter that had surrounded him then.

As usual, Jakob went to work for the day. Toward the end of the afternoon, as the gray of the sky deepened and light flakes of snow began to swirl around him, Jakob noticed a pickup truck pull up beside the makeshift guardhouse beside their work site, with extra supplies for the officers' upcoming Christmas celebration. Jakob was about to turn back to work when the label on the side of one of the boxes caught his attention.

Kerzen, it said. Candles. He wasn't sure how he knew the German word. Jakob took a deep breath. His eyes darted around the area. There were two guards a short distance away with their backs turned to him, busy smoking and talking. The other guards were keeping warm in the building the truck driver had just entered. Through a window of the building, Jakob could see the driver handing over some papers. In another few minutes, he would be coming back out and driving off with the supplies.

Quickly, Jakob picked up a small, sharp-edged rock and moved to the side of the truck. He reached out and, in a flash, used the rock to cut the thin string that held the candle box closed. He reached in and closed his fingers around a long, narrow taper. He deftly transferred it to his pants pocket and was about to reach back into the box for another when the guardhouse door opened and the driver, accompanied by a guard, stepped out.

They hurried toward Jakob. He trembled uncontrollably as he pretended to fasten the drawstring of his pants.

"Not here, you fool!" The guard slapped him hard across the back of his head. "You should know not to relieve yourself here."

"I'm sorry," Jakob stammered. "I couldn't wait."

"Filthy animal," the guard grumbled and gave him a kick that sent him sprawling on the ground. "Get back to work."

When he returned to the barrack at the end of the day, Jakob could barely drag his aching body to the bunk. Levi was already sitting there, his shoulders hunched. Jakob tried to suppress a smile as he reached into his pocket and handed Levi the candle.

"I could only get one," he said. "But I thought we might figure out how to celebrate after all."

That evening, after the last roll call, a group of inmates from the barrack huddled around the candle. Levi had cut it in half and secured the top portion to a tin plate provided by Aron's friend Antol. Levi held the bottom half of the candle in his hand.

"We will call this candle the *shamash*, the worker candle," he explained. "It is used to light the others, which are used for ceremony and prayer."

With one of Aron's precious matches, he lit the two candles and sang the traditional Hanukkah blessing. All watched the magical lighting of the candles in silence.

"In normal circumstances, we would be lighting one extra candle each night for eight days," Levi continued after the brief silence. "But for us here, the fact that we have one candle to light on the first night of Hanukkah is a miracle in itself. Even here in Auschwitz, the light of our faith can shine through."

When Jakob lifted his bowed head, he noticed with surprise that even Kapo Szekeres stood at the edge of the circle – present, though not quite joining in.

Chapter 21

A few mornings after the last day of Hanukkah, Levi announced that he could not go to their hard labor assignment that day.

"Do you realize what will happen to you?" demanded Jakob. Levi nodded and, sinking onto the edge of their bunk, he lifted off his wooden clogs. Jakob saw with horror that the bottoms of his feet were red and very swollen. Pus oozed from numerous small lacerations.

"When the Kapo punished me the other day for not standing straight enough at attention, he beat the soles of my feet. I thought they would heal, like the sores on my back did, but I guess they got infected. I just can't stand on these feet for a whole day of heavy work."

"But what are you going to do?" They both knew the hopelessness of going to the infirmary. Few people ever returned from there.

"We already had roll call. If I stay behind, maybe my absence won't be noticed till this evening. Then I can sneak into line again.

And if I get caught, let's hope that I get a beating on my back this time." Levi smiled weakly, but could not disguise the pain and fear in his eyes. Jakob could think of nothing better to suggest.

"Sit up against the wall in the corner and I'll rumple the blankets around you. Maybe the Kapo won't notice that there's still someone here when he makes the rounds."

"Thanks. Maybe if I can keep off my feet for a day and try to clean the cuts, I can be back to work tomorrow."

Jakob nodded, scared to say anything further. He was certain that without medication, without proper care, those sores would never heal.

During his work, Jakob fretted over Levi, wondering if he had been found, if his feet were healing, if he would still be there at the end of the day. All day long, Jakob couldn't stop worrying about his friend.

When they were given an unexpected break at noon and handed a slice of bread and cheese, Jakob could hardly force himself to swallow each bite. Perhaps the other prisoners had been right. Forming friendships at the camp only brought more trouble and anguish on your head.

When they trudged back to the barrack at dusk, Jakob was at the front of his line. He was the first to push open the barrack door. His eyes scanned the dim, silent building. He hurried to his bed and tossed the blankets on the floor.

Levi was gone!

"What's the matter?" Aron asked coming up behind him. They stood in grim silence contemplating the empty bed.

"Roll call!" The Kapo's shout cracked through the soft buzz of voices in the barrack. "I'll see if I can find out anything," whispered Aron as they turned to follow the others back out into the cold.

It was immediately clear that the Kapo was in a foul mood. He yelled and slapped his baton in his hand repeatedly, glaring at the rows of prisoners from under his wrinkled brows. Jakob felt the blow of the baton on his arms and back several times and from the corner of his eyes could see that Aron received the same treatment. The Kapo seemed to be picking on them in particular. Like everyone else in the barrack, he knew that they were friends with Levi. Did his treatment of them have something to do with Levi's disappearance?

While the others were dismissed and hurried to line up for their dinner rations, Aron and Jakob were ordered to remain behind, this time kneeling for an extra hour on the icy gravel. Finally, stiff and weak from the cold and hunger, and realizing that no food had been saved for them, they stumbled mutely toward their beds.

It was almost nine o'clock, lights out, when the barrack door opened and Levi reappeared. An SS officer followed him to the door and turned to have a few words with the Kapo before leaving again.

Jakob's hunger and weariness vanished at the sight of Levi. Incredibly, Levi was smiling! And on his feet, clearly visible from beneath his short pant legs, were a pair of thick woolen socks. Before any words could be exchanged, the Kapo extinguished the light and shouted "Silence!" into the blackness. Then he left them, entering his own small, private room at the front of the barrack and slamming the door shut.

Jakob and Levi waited five minutes before daring to speak in hushed whispers, their eyes adjusting to the shadowy darkness. As he lay in anxious anticipation of hearing Levi's story, Jakob became aware of a tantalizing aroma that emanated from his friend. Levi pulled a large, cloth-wrapped package from his shirt pocket.

"Here, I brought you this," were the first words he said. "For you and Aron." At the sound of his name, Aron whispered, "I'm here." He had crawled forward from his bunk and was sitting at their feet. Both he and Jakob watched spellbound as Levi lifted the flaps of cloth to expose a large chicken drumstick and a thick slice of rye bread. He ripped the bread in half and handed a piece each to Jakob and Aron. He watched as each took a large bite, then took turns removing chunks of meat from the drumstick.

Chapter 22

Levi began the account of his day. "I waited for a long time after everyone left, just in case the Kapo or someone else returned to the barracks. When I felt it was safe, I went outside and scraped some snow into my metal bowl to clean my feet. I don't know which was filthier, the snow or my feet," said Levi. "But the cold numbed my sores and I felt a bit better. I fell asleep for a while. When I awoke, the sun was streaming in through that narrow window below the roof on the opposite wall. It was shining right on me and for the first time in a very long time, I actually felt warm. I was in a small oasis of peace where, if I closed my eyes, I could pretend I was back home. I sat up and started humming to myself. Without realizing it, I must have started singing. I've always been told that I have a very good voice, and my father used to say I should become a cantor. He taught me how to read music in his spare time.

"At any rate, I must have gotten rather carried away, because all of a sudden the barrack door burst open and two SS officers stood there. *Who is that singing?*" Levi mimicked the voice with a forced accent. "Of course, I was the only one in here. I was certain that I would be severely punished, if not killed on the spot. Instead, they ordered me to follow them. When they saw I was limping, they told me to wait. One of them left and returned shortly, driving a jeep. They actually helped me in." Levi paused and grinned at Jakob's and Aron's surprised faces. "They drove me to the officers building near the main gate. When we arrived, I was still trembling with fear. They locked me in a small room, and I waited there for about half an hour until they returned with several other officers. One of them handed me some sheet music and told me to sing."

"To sing?" asked Jakob, almost choking on his bread.

Levi nodded. "Apparently, some important Nazi dignitaries are arriving here in a couple of days and the administration is planning to entertain them with a special Christmas concert. They've scraped together a whole orchestra and choir from among the prisoners. They want me to be one of the chief soloists." Jakob and Aron sat in stunned silence.

"You're going to entertain the Nazis for Christmas?" asked Aron, shaking his head.

"At least it shows they still appreciate music," said Levi. "Maybe they have some humanity left in them after all."

"Well, I don't suppose you have any choice, do you?" Aron asked.

"We always have the choice to do what is right," answered Levi. "If I had thought there was something really wrong with singing for them, I would have said no."

"And been killed on the spot, I bet."

"I will be taken to the main building for the next couple of days to practice," explained Levi. "They'll feed me there because they want me to look presentable for the performance. I can't possibly eat all the food with my stomach shrunken like it is. So I'll be able to bring extra food back for you, like I did tonight."

Jakob automatically licked his lips at the thought. Fresh bread and meat each day! It was almost impossible to imagine.

"And who knows what else I can salvage," Levi hurried on. "See these socks? Maybe I can get some for you too. When they saw me limping, they called in a doctor to clean my feet properly and bandage them. Then they gave me these socks to wear and told me I must stay off my feet for a couple of days. No roll calls for me for a while. I think someone came and talked to the Kapo about it already."

"So that's why he was in such a foul mood tonight," whispered Aron. "Not only has he been deprived of his prized victim, but you're getting all this special treatment as well. Let's hope he doesn't punish everyone because of your good fortune."

"Or come up with some new way of getting at you," said Jakob.

Chapter 23

Jakob's and Aron's lives improved over the next few days. Levi was true to his word, smuggling in food and other items to ease their circumstances. Jakob felt a slight pang of guilt at not being able to share with the other inmates. There just wasn't ever enough of anything to spread around.

"See, having friends here isn't so bad after all," Jakob remarked as he munched his way through yet another piece of bread. Both he and Aron now also had socks on their feet, soap to wash with, an undershirt to wear beneath their prisoner's garb.

"Maybe you could manage to bring us a couple of SS uniforms. Then we could pretend to be one of them and walk out of here," Aron said jokingly.

Levi saw nothing humorous in his suggestion. "That would be stealing," he said, aghast. "I would never wilfully break one of God's commandments. Everything I've given you has first been given to me. It is mine to do with as I please. They give me all this stuff so that the visiting SS dignitaries will think I am well treated. We might as well take advantage of it while we can."

"Okay." Aron held up his hand in an attempt to placate Levi. "I wasn't being serious. I wouldn't dream of getting *you* to do something dishonest. Besides, it's a totally absurd idea. No one could get away with it."

Jakob shuddered at the very thought of Aron's suggestion. Sharing Levi's bounty was dangerous enough. If Kapo Szekeres found out, they would pay for it dearly. It would indeed be absurd to take any unnecessary risks. Especially now.

Almost as important as the food and clothing Levi brought back for them was the news he learned of the outside world and the progress of the war. "The Nazis are beginning to lose. The Allied forces are advancing," Levi told them and the other inmates in an excited whisper. "The Russians from the east and American troops from the west are capturing one city after another. I know enough German to figure out, from the bits of conversations that I overhear, what is going on. That's why there's been such an influx of new prisoners and why so many more SS troops have been joining the camp. The Russians are heading this way and the Nazis are vacating the camps on their route and sending the prisoners here. They are trying to cover up their murderous activities. I've heard rumors that if the Allies can't be stopped, then soon we too will be forced to move on death marches. The news gave Jakob and the others renewed hope and determination to fight for their lives. *I've survived this long. I can hang in there for a bit longer,* Jakob encouraged himself. *The Allies must win. Soon I will get my chance to face Ivan again.*

On December 24, the ground around the barracks was frozen. A fresh layer of snow softened the harsh landscape of row upon row of gray buildings and barbed wire. Jakob shivered as he stood at attention. He worried that the tremor of his body would be noticed and that he would receive another beating. He shifted his eyes nervously in the direction of the Kapo.

But he needn't have worried. There were several SS guards, some of them obviously higher officials judging by the glittering medals adorning their overcoats. They seemed to be in a jovial mood, bantering among themselves. For once, they ignored the prisoners. That night would be Christmas Eve, and they were anticipating the feast and entertainment awaiting them. Levi had already been whisked away to the officers hall where the celebration was to be held. Jakob smiled, wondering what special treats Levi would bring back that night.

Later that day, because it was Christmas Eve and festivities were planned for the SS officers, they were ordered to return to their barracks ahead of the usual time. As he trudged back for roll call, Jakob noticed dark lumpy forms piled high beneath the Christmas tree in front of the barrack.

For a brief instant his spirits lifted. Could the guards have softened and placed gifts under the tree? Gifts of food? Parcels of canned meats, tins of vegetables and fruit, perhaps even a warm jacket for each of the prisoners?

But as he neared the tree, his knees almost buckled beneath him at the sight. He reached out an arm to grip the shoulder of the man in front of him, trying to steady himself.

There, by the dim light of the setting sun, Jakob could clearly see that those lumps were not gifts after all. They were the bodies of the men who had died that day.

Chapter 24

It was on the day after Christmas that Jakob and the other Hungarian prisoners received the best "gift" they could have hoped for. It came in the form of news translated back and forth from one language to another between prisoners. The Russian army had entered Hungary and surrounded the city of Budapest, preventing anyone from entering or leaving it.

"It's just a matter of time now before the Nazi army surrenders," Aron whispered. "They won't last long, cut off from all external supplies. Hungary will be free again." The news fortified Jakob's spirits as much as a large meal would have strengthened his body. *It can't be much longer now,* he told himself.

His thoughts turned to his longed-for encounter with Ivan. Sometimes he imagined their paths crossing in the street. Sometimes he pictured himself boldly knocking on Ivan's door. Or perhaps they would run into each other in a coffee shop. But the result was always the same. When he closed his eyes, Jakob saw himself calmly pulling up his sleeve and showing Ivan the tattooed number on his arm. He would accuse Ivan of condemning his family to a similar fate, maybe even death. But after that, the images in Jakob's mind became blurred. He was still uncertain what exact form of punishment he would inflict on Ivan.

Jakob never mentioned these daydreams to Levi. He sensed that Levi wouldn't appreciate his wish for revenge on Ivan. Aron, on the other hand, understood perfectly. He too dreamt of retaliation. Not just against one person, but against everyone who had snubbed him for being a Jew – store owners who wouldn't serve him, teachers who wouldn't respond to his upraised hand, neighbors who stood by and watched as Arrow Cross soldiers hauled him off to the trains. With Aron, Jakob plotted and planned for their return home.

Meanwhile, Levi continued to report for singing practice for a couple of hours each day. "The Christmas concert was such a success, they are now planning another celebration for New Year's Eve," he told Jakob and Aron. "With the mounting tension over the Allies' advances, the officers felt that they need another concert to lift the spirits of the guards. Again, some of us will be providing the musical entertainment. This time I have to learn some German folk songs and pop songs from the radio."

Levi was right. The tension among the guards and officers could be felt by all, manifesting itself in the form of more frequent and severe beatings, and more deaths each day. At the same time, the numbers in the barracks did not diminish. New prisoners arrived daily, dragging their emaciated bodies through the camp. Some were sent straight to the dreaded gas chambers. Despite the worsening conditions, he and Aron were determined to work harder than ever.

"We can't let them think we're useless," they told each other. "We can't give them an excuse to kill us."

Finally, December 31, the last day of 1944, arrived.

"Attention!"

They stood shivering in the chilly morning for yet another roll call. It was the third one that morning, barely an hour since they were last dismissed. There were no work detachments that day, so roll call was a convenient way to keep the prisoners occupied. They were on display for the visiting SS officers who were gathering for the evening's celebration. Kapo Szekeres strutted back and forth in front of the men, his chest out, slapping his baton in his habitual manner.

"We are going to play our game," he announced with an air of importance, glancing frequently toward the SS officers standing nearby.

"Show off," Aron hissed between his teeth. Jakob ignored the remark, his eyes glued suddenly to the Kapo's every move. Maybe, just maybe, he would be picked today. He could certainly use the treat to appease the gnawing in the pit of his stomach. Since Levi only went to practice for a couple of hours each day now, he was unable to bring back any extra food.

"We're not fed anymore," he had explained. "It's just sing and leave."

Jakob watched the Kapo as he tossed his baton into the air. It landed a couple of meters in front of one of the SS guards. The Kapo contemplated the group of prisoners. *Pick me, pick me,* Jakob pleaded in his mind. He straightened his body, hoping to be noticed. He flexed his arms and legs, ready for the run on all fours. He imagined the sweetness of the candy melting on his tongue.

For a second, the Kapo looked right at him. Then his gaze moved to Jakob's left. The Kapo pointed. The prisoner immediately dropped to all fours and scurried to get the club. Jakob watched the man pick the club up with his teeth and hurry back to place it at the Kapo's feet. As the eager man knelt and begged, his tongue hanging out for his reward, the SS soldiers erupted with laughter and cheering.

Encouraged by their response, the Kapo tried again. Once again, he threw the club. This time, Jakob noticed a vicious smile playing around the corners of the Kapo's mouth. His eyes took on a steely glint that Jakob had learned to dread. Jakob held his breath, no longer sure if he wanted to be chosen. And then the unexpected happened.

For the first time since his arrival, it was Levi whom the Kapo pointed at. Unlike the previous prisoner, who had immediately sprung into action, Levi did not move.

There was a moment of deathly silence. Jakob's heart pounded painfully in his chest. *Go, you idiot,* he silently urged.

Nothing happened.

"Number 22741," the Kapo yelled out the full number tattooed on Levi's arm. Levi stepped forward and faced the Kapo.

"Fetch!" the Kapo ordered, pointing at the club lying on the ground. Levi straightened his body and held his head high. For an instant, Jakob saw the proud, tall man who had first marched into camp.

"If God had wanted me to be like an animal, then he would have given me four feet," Levi said with a loud, firm voice. "But God made me a man. And, with the dignity of a man, I will walk as I am meant to do." He turned toward the club lying a short distance away.

Before he could take a single step, a gunshot split the deadly silence. Levi's body crumpled to the ground and a pool of red blood stained the white snow around his head. Grinning, an SS officer wiped the barrel of his pistol on his sleeve.

Chapter 25

There was no opportunity to react. No chance to run and kneel beside Levi's body. The SS officer with the smoking pistol pointed it at another prisoner.

"Fetch!" he yelled. The man, fearing for his life, immediately scampered toward the baton, right over Levi's twisted legs.

Jakob's numbness as they returned to the barrack had little to do with the cold. Only with Aron's prodding did Jakob manage to get inside, where he slumped down on the edge of his bunk. He could still see the SS officers slapping Kapo Szekeres on the back, congratulating him on the fine entertainment he had provided.

"Those idiots," said Aron, sinking down beside Jakob. "They have no idea that they just destroyed their top entertainment for this evening. I wonder if the Kapo knew what he was doing. His wife and son are assured of a long life after this."

"And Levi," said Jakob. "I think Levi knew exactly what he was doing. He knew what the consequences of his words would be."

Jakob and Aron sat in silence, side by side, their hands clasped between their knees, not daring to look at each other, not wanting to see each other's tears. They were so upset, they didn't even bother lining up for the weak soup and slice of bread offered at lunch.

The day passed in a haze. Jakob couldn't think. *Levi is gone,* he kept telling himself, trying to make the reality take hold in his being. Levi's presence, his influence on Jakob, had been so strong. How could it come to such a sudden, tragic end?

Throughout the day, Levi's body remained on the ground. No one was ordered to remove it. No one was permitted to go near it. Jakob had seen many corpses since he had arrived at the camp. While the first few had shocked and horrified him, by now he had become used to the sight. He had learned to barricade his feelings from what he saw. He had learned not to react. Not seeing was an essential tool of survival at the camp.

But not this time. Levi had been his friend, and the sight of his twisted body churned Jakob's emotions more than anything else he had experienced. He understood why the other prisoners had reservations about forming close friendships.

Yet Jakob did not regret their friendship. He was glad to have been Levi's friend. Through him, Jakob had rediscovered his Jewish identity. He had learned that it was something to be proud of, not something to hide. No, Jakob did not regret his friendship with Levi, only the emptiness he felt in his soul now that Levi was gone.

Later that night, with his lips set in grim determination, Jakob rose from his bunk. He snuck past the Kapo's closed door and eased his way out of the barrack. Stepping lightly in order to avoid crunching the hard-packed snow, he made his way to Levi's body. A thin layer of fresh snow had fallen, covering and erasing all traces of the red stain around his head. Gently, Jakob covered Levi's face and body with the blanket he had brought with him. Snatches of raucous laughter drifted in the air from the direction of the officers building. But around Jakob, all was still.

He knelt beside Levi and quietly recited *Kaddish*, the prayer for the dead. Levi had taught him this Hebrew prayer. Some evenings before going to sleep, they had recited it together for the prisoners who had lost their lives that day. Now Jakob said it for his friend Levi.

PART THREE

Chapter 26

January 2, 1945

As the prisoners were about to depart for their work assignments, a large army truck pulled up and SS soldiers disembarked. After a brief dialogue with the guards, the soldiers began selecting men from among the prisoners. Those selected were ordered to the back of one of the trucks. Jakob and Aron exchanged concerned looks. Were the chosen prisoners being carted off to be killed? Jakob noticed that only the fittest men were being picked – if, after months of deprivation, anyone could be called fit.

"Perhaps they are being selected for a special work crew," he whispered to Aron. It had happened before. Prisoners had been sent off to distant work sites where rapid cleanup or reconstruction was required. At such times, he and Aron had slouched and averted their eyes, not wanting to be chosen. They had been frightened that an even worse fate might await them. That was not the case now. Since Levi's death, both Jakob and Aron were desperate to get away from Kapo Szekeres, from the barrack, from Auschwitz.

Both Jakob and Aron straightened themselves out, puffing out their chests and squaring their shoulders. They caught the eye of one of the soldiers and both were ordered to get into the back of the truck.

"This will be our first step toward going home," Jakob vowed, his confidence restored. A few more prisoners were ordered in, followed by two guards with guns at the ready. The back doors slammed shut and the truck rumbled off.

Since there were no windows or openings in the back of the truck, Jakob had no idea as to which direction they were traveling in. And he had no idea why they'd been taken. The guards gave no explanation. They just glared at the prisoners as if daring them to make a sound. Jakob began to wonder if he and Aron had made the right choice.

After an anxious journey, the truck finally came to an abrupt halt. The doors swung open and the prisoners were ordered to get out. The sun was still high in the sky, so they couldn't have been in the truck for more than two or three hours, Jakob guessed. They were still in Poland.

"You are in Arbeitslager Blechhammer," one of the officers explained in German as they all assembled. "This is a satellite camp of Auschwitz, an industrial complex with a synthetic oil facility." His tone was proud as he described the camp. "About a week ago, our enemies bombed part of the complex. You have been brought here to clear away the rubble and retrieve whatever can be saved. The prisoners already here are needed to continue the work in the rest of the camp. Roll calls will be conducted each morning and evening, as usual. You will begin work immediately. Any breaking of the rules, any slacking off at work, will result in immediate death." His words were translated by another officer into broken Hungarian and Polish.

The words were ominous, but Jakob tried to remain optimistic. At least it was not Auschwitz. There was a different Kapo from the hated Kapo Szekeres. He and Aron shared the same bunk and they could talk when not being watched. Their new barrack was smaller than the one at Auschwitz, but just as crowded. The food was just as scarce, though somewhat better. There were more vegetables in the broth, and occasionally a rare lump of meat to give them strength. Their new Kapo was a tall, sullen man of few words. As long as the prisoners behaved, he seemed to leave them alone.

As at Auschwitz, they were awakened before dawn and counted. After breakfast they were immediately marched to the bombed site. Their route brought them close to the outer fence of the camp and Jakob had his first glimpse of the open countryside with its forests, fields, and scattered houses, smoke curling from their chimneys. How peaceful this winter landscape seemed. Did the people in those houses know what was happening just a short distance down their road?

Clearing the wreckage of office buildings, holding tanks, and mangled pipes and chimneys was hard work, harder than Jakob could have imagined. But there were unexpected benefits. Amid the still-smoldering rubble were hidden treasures. Shirts, sweaters, and shoes that could be retrieved from corpses. There were odd bits of food to be found, an onion or carrot, maybe even a hardened loaf of moldy bread unearthed from beneath the bricks of a former kitchen. Sometimes they found old, torn pages of newspaper, or cardboard.

Smuggling these items back to the barracks was relatively easy beneath their loose prison uniforms. The SS guards, with their guns and clubs always at the ready, stayed on the periphery of the bombed area, unwilling to venture into the unstable ruins and foul fumes. And though the prisoners were searched at the end of each day, the guards here were only interested in confiscating found weapons or truly valuable items.

Within a couple of days, Jakob managed to find a sweater that he could wear beneath his shirt. He stuffed newspaper into the tips of his wooden clogs for extra warmth for his frostbitten toes. He wrapped bits of torn cloth around his hands in an effort to protect his oozing blisters. When he found food, he consumed it ravenously, on the spot.

All that mattered now, as far as Jakob was concerned, was to stay alive and return home. The memory of his discussions with Levi, the traditions and prayers he had learned, only brought tears to his eyes and made his throat constrict painfully whenever he thought of them. It was less painful to focus on getting back home and confronting

Ivan. He kept reminding himself that it was Ivan's fault that he was here having to endure all this suffering. If Ivan had been like Levi, if he'd had courage, he would have stood up to his father.

Chapter 27

After a week of digging through the rubble at the new camp, Jakob came upon two SS corpses buried beneath a large sheet of metal. Their frozen faces were those of young men, barely older than Levi had been. One had a deep gash across his forehead, possibly caused by the sheet of metal. The other's neck was twisted at an unnatural angle.

At first Jakob turned away with disgust, hoping someone else from his team of workers would be forced to deal with the bodies. But then a comment that Aron had made not so long ago surfaced in his mind. *Maybe you could manage to bring us a couple of SS uniforms. Then we could pretend to be one of them and walk out of here.* It had been said in jest at the time, but now the possibility of such a plan started to spin through Jakob's head. Could it work? What if he was discovered? He would be killed on the spot or worse. He recalled the images of stiff, naked, dangling bodies, beaten black and blue, or entombed in ice or riddled with bullets, displayed for all to see. What if that happened to him? Was it worth the risk?

But they probably wouldn't last much longer at this camp. As it became clear that the Nazis were losing the war, camps and work sites were evacuated and prisoners were sent on death marches by the Nazis. They were marched for hundreds of kilometers across the frozen land. It was doubtful that in their emaciated condition many would survive. Rumors had circulated through their barrack that as soon as their cleanup mission was complete, they too, would be sent on their way.

Jakob looked at the corpses, their uniforms. Time for thinking about it was running out. He made up his mind.

Jakob's heart pounded as he shook Aron's shoulder later that night and whispered in his ear. "I have a plan. We are going to escape!" He had waited impatiently until the snores of the other prisoners had become a monotonous background rumble before daring to wake Aron.

Aron woke instantly and propped himself up on his elbows. "What are you talking about?"

"It was your idea, really," said Jakob, explaining to Aron about finding the bodies that day. "I built a barricade around them from the rubble. Then I waited till the others in my group were preoccupied with their particular messes and I was sure I wouldn't be seen. Bit by bit, I stripped the uniforms off the soldiers. It was difficult. They were so stiff. But I did it. I got their boots and caps. Everything."

Aron shook his head. "I was joking when I suggested escaping. We could never pull it off. And you know what happens to people who are caught. We've seen their punishment enough times."

Jakob's doubts surfaced again. If Aron thought it was too risky, how could they possibly succeed? But then he thought of Gabor, of Levi, of all the others who had been ruthlessly murdered at the whim of SS or Arrow Cross officers. If they escaped now, maybe he and Aron would survive. With the Russian and American forces coming closer, the war might be over soon.

"You've heard the rumors," he said, more determined. "Do you want to go on one of those death marches? You said yourself that we would never live through it." Aron made no response. Jakob continued, "I hid the uniforms inside one of those long, wide pipes that are littered all over the place. Tomorrow we'll put on the uniforms and walk out as officers. It will be hours before they notice that we're gone – not until roll call." Jakob knew he made it sound simpler than it would be, but he needed to convince Aron.

"Let me think about it," Aron said, yawning. "Right now I want to sleep. We can talk about it tomorrow." He twisted on his elbow and lay his head down again, his back to Jakob.

"We don't have time," Jakob persisted, grabbing a hold of Aron's shoulder. "My work group is almost finished clearing the roadway. Tomorrow or the next day I might get moved. Or someone else might find those uniforms. We have to act right away. It's our only chance."

"You mean it's *your* only chance. You can go ahead and try. You don't need *me* to go with you. Ask someone else." Aron shrugged off Jakob's hand. His response took Jakob by surprise. He had never considered escaping on his own. If he had found only one body, had only one uniform, the possibility of escape wouldn't have entered his mind.

"I don't want to ask someone else," he said after a moment. "I need *you*. I know you. I trust you. I admit that it's a crazy, dangerous plan. And there is the chance we'll get caught. That's why I'm too frightened to try it alone," he admitted. "I need your help. My previous plans always messed up. You're good at this kind of thing. You can think quickly on your feet. Together, we're strong. We'll fight them if we have to."

"Not if they have guns," Aron interrupted Jakob's flow of words, but Jakob pressed on.

"One of us can keep guard when the other sleeps. Together, we have more of a chance. I'm willing to try only if you are. I don't want to die here." Aron was silent for so long that Jakob feared he had fallen asleep. But then, in the dense darkness, he heard Aron's voice.

"I wonder what it would be like to sleep on a real bed again? To be warm, not to be hungry, to feel safe. To see my family. Maybe you are right. Maybe this could work. And," he chuckled, "even Levi would approve. We're not stealing those uniforms. The dead officers have no more use for them. All right," he said finally, turning back to face Jakob in the darkness of the night. "I will go with you. I will make sure you survive."

Chapter 28

It was clear to Jakob that once Aron had agreed, he was fully committed. They spent most of the night whispering their plans. Their first challenge was to figure out how they would meet up. Jakob's work unit was assigned to removing mangled machinery from a roadway that bisected the refinery grounds. Aron's group was clearing out a partially collapsed building some distance away.

"Just walk over, as if that is what you are supposed to be doing," Jakob suggested. "If you are stopped, say that you need a crowbar and have been told that my group has one to spare." Aron considered this too vague, but he had nothing better to offer. There were many unresolved problems that they would need to figure out, but the most important thing, Aron and Jakob agreed, was that they had the uniforms. If they could wear them like men with authority, then they could walk among the other guards undetected. It was a big "if"!

Snow swirled down around the prisoners during the pre-dawn roll call. For once, Jakob was oblivious to the cold. He was too preoccupied with what he and Aron were about to do. Thankfully, roll call in this camp was brief. There was too much work to be done. After a hasty breakfast of weak tea, a slice of bread, and a slab of cheese, they walked along paths and roads to the bombed sites. Each work group was accompanied to their designated location by several guards. But once there, the guards fell back, content to patrol the periphery of each area, smoking and talking among themselves. They were armed and confident that none of the prisoners could get past them. The sun was just about to rise over the horizon. The ground and the ruins were cloaked in dark shadows, shadows that would help to conceal a moving body.

Jakob and Aron knew that they had to act quickly to take advantage of the dim morning light. It was too early for the guards to be bored or to start looking for diversion by harassing the workers.

As soon as he arrived at his work site, Jakob busied himself near one end of the long hollow pipe that concealed the uniforms, hoping that it wouldn't be long before Aron turned up. Jakob had had the foresight the previous day to pile large pieces of warped metal at both ends of the pipe, to block him and Aron from direct observation. To his relief, it wasn't long before he saw Aron walking toward him with a purposeful gait. After a quick, nervous glance to make sure that no one was watching, Jakob crawled inside the wide pipe. Within seconds, Aron followed.

Jakob proceeded cautiously in the dark on hands and knees until his hands encountered the fabric of a uniform. He picked it up, felt the length, found a zipper. It must be a pair of trousers. He passed it to Aron.

"Here, put this on." His hands located the other pair of trousers and in the cramped space Jakob maneuvered himself onto his back. He slipped off his prisoner pants and wiggled into the uniform's pant legs. Aron's grunts let him know that he was doing the same. Next, Jakob's hands felt for lighter fabric, small buttons, and a collar. He handed the shirt to Aron and groped around for its partner. Putting it on was far trickier than the pants, especially in the tight space. Jakob's arm found a sleeve and slipped into it.

Jakob fumbled around for the next piece of clothing, worrying that they were taking far too long. "Here's a tie. This should be a lot easier. I didn't undo the knot so you can just slip the noose over your head and tighten it."

"A little foretaste of what might be in store for us if this doesn't work, eh?" joked Aron. Jakob ignored the remark and shoved a jacket in Aron's face.

"Let's deal with the socks and boots outside," he said once his own jacket was on. "It's too cramped in here." Without waiting for a reply, he rolled over onto his front and, pushing the boots in front of him, crawled out of the pipe. He was relieved to see that the sky had brightened only slightly. Large flakes of snow were still drifting down. Jakob sat just inside the bottom edge of the pipe, his legs dangling as he pulled on the socks and then the boots. The boots were too large, and he wondered how he would be able to run in them.

At last he stood up and almost collapsed with fright when he noticed an SS guard straightening his cap at the other end of the tunnel. He laughed with relief when he realized it was Aron.

"You look like the real thing," Jakob said, impressed.

"Well, you don't." Aron hurried over and straightened Jakob's tie and the lapel of his jacket. He placed a cap on Jakob's head at just the angle that the officers wore them. "And here, in your rush to get out, you forgot these." He reached back and retrieved a belt, which he fastened around Jakob's waist. Attached to it was a rubber club dangling by a short rope and a holster with a pistol. Jakob felt foolish to have made such a grave mistake. Aron was already wearing his own belt, club, and pistol.

"See, I told you I couldn't do this on my own," Jakob said.

"By the way, do you know if there are any bullets in these?" Aron asked, pointing at the pistols.

Jakob shook his head. "Let's hope we don't have to find out." Aron took a step back and each boy regarded the other.

"It's a good thing we decided to keep our sweaters on under the uniforms," he said. "They're still rather loose, but hopefully no one will notice. This snow should help." The large flakes had settled on their uniforms and did not melt, helping to camouflage the many creases and stains.

Aron gave a final nod of approval. "I think we're ready. Remember! We are bold men. Officers. Let's act like them!" They headed out of the rubble toward the cleared road.

Chapter 29

They walked with what they hoped was an air of confidence down the roadway. Aron insisted that they walk slowly as if inspecting the cleanup crews along the way. He even shouted orders and insults at the crews in German. Over the months they had both learned a fair bit of German, and Aron, who seemed to have a flair for languages, had also picked up bits of Polish, Ukrainian – whatever he heard spoken by the other prisoners. In each of these languages, his accent was perfect. It all came in handy now.

The oil refinery was spread out over a large area. While there were no barbed-wire fences or lookout towers, it was heavily guarded by SS soldiers stationed every few feet around the periphery and somewhat more sporadically along the cleared roadways. Jakob and Aron passed one soldier after another, their hearts pounding in their chests. But the guards only gave them a cursory, uninterested glance. Jakob was beginning to believe that their preposterous scheme was going to work after all, when Aron made a ridiculously risky move.

They had come to the intersection of two roads where a patrol car had been left idling without a driver. Aron hesitated. He held up his palm to caution Jakob and scrutinized the area around them.

"Those guards there," Aron pointed at some soldiers a short distance away, "they don't look like this car would belong to them, do they?" he asked.

"No," Jakob replied, not sure why Aron had paused. "They are just watching those prisoners clear the bricks around that collapsed wall. But never mind them. We'd better keep moving and get out of here."

"Quick, get in!" Aron hissed.

"What are you talking about?"

"Get in the car!" Aron commanded again. "We'll drive our way out of here."

"You're crazy. They'll come after us. We'll get caught for sure."

"Look around. Do you see any other vehicles nearby? How will they catch us? On foot?" Aron opened the door as he spoke. He jumped into the driver's seat. There was no time to think. Unless he wanted to be left behind, Jakob had no choice. He scrambled in beside Aron.

"Do you even know how to drive?" Jakob asked, incredulous.

"My uncle used to let me take the wheel of his car. He showed me how the gear stick works. I can handle this." Aron grinned as he struggled with the gearshift and the car lurched forward. The guards turned to look at them, but didn't seem either concerned or surprised. Aron saluted them as they passed. He rolled down his window. "We have an urgent errand. Tell the other driver that we'll have his car back in a minute," he called out in German and quickly rolled his window back up. They zigzagged from side to side for a bit before Aron got the car under control. Jakob glanced nervously out the back window, but there was no one pursuing them.

Aron drove toward a water tower that had somehow survived the bombing. It was their sole landmark in this mangled landscape. The main road leading away from the refinery passed right by it.

"This is the direction toward the camp's main entrance," Jakob pointed out. "Our plan was to go the other way. We were going to take the side road that winds close to the forest."

"I know. But we assumed that we would be on foot and would need to disappear into the woods as soon as possible. Now that we have a car, we don't need to do that," said Aron. "There are a couple of crossroads past the gate. I overheard one officer giving directions to another a few days ago. He said that the road to the left goes toward Ostrava. Ostrava is on the way to the Hungarian border. We'll go that way."

Jakob slumped against the seat, distraught by the rapid unraveling of their carefully made plan. What was Aron doing? He was going to get them killed. This had been a horrible idea after all. They should have stayed put. What had ever possessed him to think that Aron could help him escape?

In the distance, Jakob could see the barricade that the SS guards had put across the road leading out of the refinery compound. Every vehicle and person passing in or out was stopped and inspected. Aron hadn't taken that into consideration when he'd decided to steal this vehicle. The groups of soldiers on either side of the barricade were huddled together, their collars turned up against the snow, waiting for the car to approach and stop. But Aron continued to drive at the same speed. He showed no indication that he intended to slow down, let alone stop. Was he planning to smash through the barricade? That would be certain death. They were sure to be shot at and pursued.

Jakob sat up. He wasn't about to let that happen. He looked over at Aron sitting straight and proud in his uniform, a grim determination on his face. Jakob looked down at his own uniform. His eyes widened and he suddenly knew what he needed to do. Jakob quickly rolled down his window and leaned out almost to his waist.

"Move, you idiots!" he shouted in his best German, waving his arms. "This is an emergency!" Several soldiers jumped at the command, took one look at the rapidly approaching car, at the officer gesturing and yelling out the window, and swiftly moved the wooden barrier just as Aron roared the vehicle through. The other soldiers stood at attention, saluting. Shaking, Jakob collapsed back onto his seat. Aron laughed and looked at Jakob with amazement.

"That was brilliant! Whatever possessed you to do that?" he asked. "I was going to crash through that barricade. We couldn't afford to be questioned. I never thought they would take orders from us like that, without hesitation."

"Our uniforms," said Jakob, panting to ease the rapid beating of his heart. "Look at our stripes. We are their superior officers. They wouldn't dare question our orders. I don't think anyone will chase us for a while."

"So who is it who thinks quickly on his feet now?" asked Aron.

Chapter 30

Go! Go! Go! Jakob wished he could will Aron to go faster. But Aron was reluctant to drive too fast and risk losing control of the vehicle. Jakob figured that they had been driving for about fifteen minutes. He resisted the impulse to turn around and glance out the back window yet again. It made Aron nervous and he swerved every time Jakob turned. So far there had been no sign of pursuit and they had only passed one other army vehicle traveling in the opposite direction. But their slow and steady pace was maddening.

When they came to the crossroads, Aron hesitated. He looked in both directions. "If they come after us, they will probably assume that we would head toward Ostrava. But down this other road I can see a forest in the distance. We can abandon the car there and hide in the woods till nightfall, then carry on by foot."

Jakob was silent for a moment, considering. Aron was right. The main thing was for them to stay hidden and then get out of occupied Poland as soon as possible. Hungary – home – was to the south. As long as they headed in that general direction without getting caught, it didn't matter what route they took.

Jakob nodded his agreement.

They traveled in silence for a while, passing through flat farmland dotted with tiny houses. Smoke curled out of the chimneys. But it soon became evident that the peacefulness of the countryside was deceptive. Every mile or so they noticed a corpse, sometimes several corpses, in the ditch at the side of the road.

Jakob shuddered. He looked down at his uniform. If he were to die, he didn't want to be wearing a Nazi uniform. He did not want to be identified with the cruelty that the uniform represented. "We need to get rid these uniforms as well," he said to Aron.

"I'm more concerned about finding food," said Aron as he pulled over to the side of the road. They had arrived at the edge of the forest. "We won't get too far without something to eat. Who knows how big that forest is."

"We have the pistols," Jakob said, "Perhaps we can kill a rabbit or something – though I've never killed anything before," he added quietly.

As Jakob climbed out of the car, he noticed a small brown paper bag on the floor in front of the rear seat. He opened the back door and took it out. Inside were a fresh roll, a thick slab of meat wrapped in paper, a red apple, and two cookies. Jakob's eyes bulged in surprise and his mouth watered. With shaking hands he showed his find to Aron. It was difficult to control their urge to devour the food right there, but their safety had to come first. They deflated one of the car tires so that the abandoned car wouldn't seem strange to anyone passing by. With pine branches that they broke off a nearby tree, they did their best to erase their footprints behind them as they headed into the forest.

"The falling snow will finish the job for us," said Aron with satisfaction.

The snow was not very deep beneath the trees, barely reaching past their ankles, so they walked quickly. After a few minutes, Jakob stopped. He couldn't wait any longer.

"This is far enough for now. Let's eat." They sat on a fallen tree trunk and after splitting the roll and meat in half, consumed their feast. For a fleeting moment they considered saving the apple and cookies for later, but were unable to resist the temptation.

"We made it!" grinned Jakob, when they finished. Now that his ravishing hunger had been appeased, he was more optimistic.

"Not yet," Aron cautioned. "We still have hundreds of miles to cover by foot without being found by the enemy and without more food. But yes," he finally conceded with a smile, "we have done okay so far."

Within a few hours, they reached the far edge of the forest where it opened onto snow-covered fields crisscrossed by wooden rail fences.

In the distance, a barn roof peeked over a low hilltop. After a brief discussion, they decided it was best to stay beneath the shelter of the trees during the day and to travel under the dark protection of night. Jakob showed Aron how they could pile up the snow between two trees and fashion a makeshift shelter. It was something Ivan had taught him one winter when they were pretending to be hunters in the far north.

When the shelter was complete, they huddled close together for warmth and took turns trying to sleep. Though it was only mid-day, after their sleepless night of planning, they were both exhausted. Earlier, they had examined the pistols and found that Aron's gun held two bullets while Jakob's had only one. In their pants pockets, they had each found a thin wallet containing some Polish money. In the inside pockets of their jackets were some identity papers.

"The money could come in handy, though it doesn't look like much," said Aron. "But the identity papers will only get us into extra trouble. Look," he pointed to some words and numbers, "they are for men who don't look anything like us. If anyone should examine them we would be caught in our lie." They tore up the papers into tiny bits and hid them beneath a log.

Jakob was the first to keep watch. He held the pistol propped on his knees, alert to the slightest sound, hoping he would never have to use it, but ready for anything. When it was his turn to rest, he slept fitfully, aware of every sound, every movement of the wind.

Once the night was well upon them, they got on their way. At first Jakob felt conspicuous out in the open field. They were two black dots in an expanse of white. It had stopped snowing, the clouds had scattered, and billions of stars twinkled overhead.

Jakob stopped and spread his arms wide heavenward. For the first time, he felt free! There was no barbed wire in sight. No chimneys spewed out their putrid smoke of death. No Kapo or SS guard ordered him around, ready to shoot or give a beating. Jakob breathed deep. Despite the present cold and the hunger, despite the difficulties ahead, he was grateful to be here. He looked at the fresh, glittering snow around him. He took another deep breath, just happy to be alive.

As he trudged on, trying to keep up with Aron, he thought of all he had lost – his home, his parents, his aunt, his cousins, his friendship with Ivan, his attachment to Levi. *It must be for some greater purpose,* he assured himself. *All that I have suffered and have seen others suffer – maybe I can turn it around and do some good.*

But first, he had something important to take care of. If he was going to be able to leave all that had happened behind him, he would need to deal with Ivan, first and foremost.

Chapter 31

After several hours of trudging, Jakob and Aron could see a farmhouse a short distance from a barn, and a dark ribbon of road beyond it. A barn and a house meant the possibility of food and the opportunity to discard their SS uniforms. They advanced cautiously. Jakob wished that the stars and the moon weren't quite so bright. However, there seemed to be no one around to notice. The windows of the house were dark. Either the occupants were asleep, or the house was empty.

They went into the barn and paused in the open doorway until their eyes adjusted to the dark interior. It appeared to be empty. There was no stomping or shuffling of hooves or the heavy breathing of farm animals. They felt their way cautiously along the wall until their feet bumped into a pile of hay.

"You stay here and wait," said Aron. "I'll see if I can get into the house and get us some food and a change of clothes."

"No. I'm coming with you. It might take both of us to deal with whoever is in there."

"We'll make more noise together. If I get into trouble, I will need you to rescue me later. If we both get caught, we can't help each other." Jakob reluctantly agreed. He followed Aron back to the barn door, but remained in its shadows as Aron, with his gun drawn, slowly approached the house. Jakob saw the back door open and Aron disappear inside.

Jakob waited, straining to hear the slightest sound coming from the house, but there was nothing. No lights turned on. There was no indication of a commotion.

Finally the back door of the house opened again and Aron emerged. He was carrying something bulky in his arms.

"Well, that was easy," Aron exhaled as he arrived back at the barn. "Tense, but easy. The back door was unlocked and inside I saw and heard no one. Whoever lives here was either asleep upstairs or has left. This coat, the two sweaters, and hat were hanging on a hook by the back door so I grabbed them. Look, I got a pair of gloves too."

"What about food?" interrupted Jakob. "Did you get any food?" They had not eaten since they had shared the contents of the paper bag from the car that morning. Aron smiled and pulled half a loaf of bread from beneath the coat that he had dropped on the ground. He handed it to Jakob. He reached into his pants pockets, pulling out four eggs from one and a small jar from the other.

"Preserves," he said. "I think they're plums." Jakob dropped to his knees, ripped the loaf in half and bit into one piece. "This time we should save some for later," suggested Aron as he too, took a bite of bread. "And we'll save two of the eggs for later as well," he added with his mouth full. "They're not cooked but they will have to do."

Jakob nodded as he took an egg, broke it and let the contents of the shells drip into his upturned, open mouth. Its rawness did not bother him. It was food. He was sorry that it slid down his throat so quickly. Aron opened the jar of plums and they took turns pulling the sweet, juicy fruits from the jar. When the plums were all gone they shared the remaining liquid.

Jakob looked toward the house. "Do you think you could go back for more?" he asked.

Aron hesitated, then shook his head. "No. There wasn't much else I could find without a light. We should get going." They took off their SS jackets, keeping on their shirts and pants. "I thought we could take turns wearing the coat and sweaters," explained Aron. "One of us can wear the two heavy sweaters and the other the thick coat." Jakob chose to wear the sweaters first. Since the coat had a hood, he also got the knitted hat. Aron put the remainder of their food and one of the pistols into the coat's large pockets. Jakob kept his gun in his pants pocket. After stuffing the SS uniform jackets under the straw, they left the safety of the barn.

As they walked toward the road, Jakob hesitated. "Wait here a minute," he said and without explanation ran to the back door of the house. Quickly he searched the area and, detecting a small woodpile nearby, grabbed one of the logs. He then reached into his pocket and removed the money from the wallet. After securing the bills under the log on the back step, he ran back to Aron.

"I feel better now," he said, remembering Levi. "It didn't feel right taking other people's food and clothes and leaving nothing in return. Even if whoever lives there is gone now, they might return and miss what we took." Aron grunted and shook his head and they continued their trek to the road. Soon the narrow dirt road crossed another more major one. Looking to the stars and the moon to guide their course, Jakob and Aron turned south.

They walked for most of the night, jumping into a ditch or hiding behind a tree whenever a vehicle approached. But, thankfully, those occasions were rare. By the time the morning light forced them to stop, both of them were limping. Though the socks and boots were a great improvement over the wooden clogs they had been forced to wear in the camp, their feet were covered in open sores from months of abuse. Jakob felt he could not last another step.

They hid behind the walls of what remained of a stone farmhouse. Its roof and contents had been burned, as had the adjoining barn. They assumed it had been the work of the conquering German army. After eating the remainder of their bread and eggs, they again took turns sleeping and keeping guard.

Day after day, they traveled in this fashion, walking at night, sleeping by day, pilfering bits of food whenever the opportunity arose. They stayed away from towns and people, uncertain whom they could trust. Jakob lost track of the number of days they had been on the road. All he knew was that they were steadily heading south, toward Hungary and home. They had discarded their guns, having used the bullets on rabbits after going without food for several days. They had climbed over hills and had crossed swift-flowing streams. Occasionally they heard the sounds of battles raging in the distance. Fighter planes flew overhead, their exhaust leaving trails that remained in the sky long after the planes had passed.

As they walked, Aron talked of the family he hoped to be reunited with in Debrecen. Perhaps they had survived. Perhaps they were waiting for him. Jakob couldn't talk of his family, at least not about seeing them again. He doubted that either his mother or father were still alive. He just couldn't imagine them surviving the horrors of a concentration camp. Instead, he told Aron about summers spent at Lake Balaton, going fishing with his father, reading books out loud to Mother in the shade of the large walnut tree.

Then, one night, after they left yet another forest and started out along a fresh road, Jakob and Aron noticed that the language on the road signs had changed. They had entered Slovakia. Knowing that Slovakia had joined with Germany early in the war and had helped the Nazi army invade Poland, they became even more cautious.

Everywhere they looked, they saw destruction around them. In many places, even the forests had been burned. Remaining hidden among the charred trunks became an almost impossible task. They wondered about the progress of the war. They had heard no news since leaving Auschwitz. What was happening in Slovakia now? Had Hungary been liberated? How far had the Allies progressed?

They had also lost track of time. Jakob only knew that it had been days since they had last eaten anything other than handfuls of snow. In their weakened state, they covered less and less distance each night. Finally, one day, well before the sky began to turn a lighter shade of gray, they collapsed behind some fallen tree trunks at the side of the road, unable to walk deeper into the shelter of the woods. Despite his best efforts to stay awake, Jakob, whose turn it was to keep watch, dozed off.

Chapter 32

When Jakob opened his eyes, he saw that the sun had climbed high above the horizon. But it was not the sun's glare that had awakened him. It was the voices of men. He and Aron were surrounded by a troop of soldiers.

Aron woke up as well, and the two of them scrambled to their feet. Three guns were aimed at their chests. One of the soldiers shouted a question in a language Jakob did not understand. It did not matter. He was too frightened, too discouraged to speak. They had failed.

The question was repeated, but this time in a different language.

"Who are you?" Jakob finally understood the words when the question was asked a third time, this time in broken Hungarian. His mind was too muddled to think of a response that might possibly save them. He glanced at Aron for help.

It was then that he noticed the line of army vehicles parked at the side of the road. He saw the small flags displayed on their hood.

They were Russian flags! These were Allies!

"We are Hungarian," he said, pushing up the sleeve of his jacket to display the numbers tattooed on his arm. "We escaped from Auschwitz."

The guns were lowered and, in their place, hands reached toward them. Instinctively, Jakob cowered. But the hands that touched him were supportive. Helpful arms wrapped around him.

"We are friends. We are with the Russian army," said the soldier who had first spoken to them in Hungarian. "You are safe now. We have driven the Germans out. We are here to help."

A soldier hurried over from one of the trucks with blankets, which he wrapped around Jakob and Aron. Another soldier extended a hand with bread for each of them, followed by cups of hot tea from a thermos. Forgetting all else, Jakob grabbed the bread and stuffed his mouth. He winced as a sip of the scalding liquid burned his cracked lips. The soldiers watched in silence as he and Aron ravenously consumed the bread and tea.

Jakob and Aron looked at each other. Could this be true? Relief swept over Jakob. They were safe. There would be no more hiding and fearing for their lives. He was truly free to go home! Both he and Aron hugged their liberators, their eyes brimming with tears.

The soldiers helped them up into the back of a truck. Inside, there were six other refugees – two women and four men – who greeted them with weary smiles. Two soldiers hopped in and more food was passed around. Jakob and Aron were told that they were being taken to a displaced persons camp for refugees in Austria. With much of Hungary still under German occupation, this camp would be, for the time being, a safe place for them. There, one of the soldiers explained, they would be treated by doctors, fed, bathed, and given fresh clothing.

Jakob and Aron also learned that two days before, on January 27, 1945, the Russian troops had liberated Auschwitz.

It was early May when Jakob finally arrived in Buda by train. He and Aron had stayed at the refugee camp for several months – slowly regaining their strength and allowing their bodies to heal. Though accommodations at the refugee camp were simple, they had plenty of food every day, warm clothes, and no more hard labor. It mattered little to Jakob that he shared a large army tent with several other people. After all, he had a whole cot all to himself.

Once his flesh filled out again and the old vitality returned to his limbs, once all the sores on his feet and hands had healed, Jakob grew restless. The war in Europe was officially over. The last of the Nazi troops had been driven out of Hungary on April 4. It was time to leave. It was time to return and face Ivan.

"We should be on our way," he said to Aron on a sunny spring morning. We are wasting our time here." Aron agreed.

"Even here they assume that you are older than you really are," said Aron. "We can ask to be assigned as chaperones to the next group of children who are being transported back across the border to Hungary. I heard talk that there is a busload being organized to leave later this week."

Both Jakob and Aron were chosen to accompany the group of unnaturally solemn and quiet children. All of them were young survivors of concentration camps. Jakob's heart ached as he helped to minister to their various needs along the way. He wondered what sort of future awaited them. How many still had a living parent eager to be reunited with them? While he was occupied with the children, he was able to keep at bay his anxieties about his own uncertain future.

Shortly after crossing the border from Slovakia into Hungary, Jakob and Aron parted at a makeshift Red Cross station where the children were to stay. It was time to go their separate ways – Jakob to continue on toward Budapest by train and Aron to Debrecen. They bade each other awkward good-byes, knowing that the period of time they had shared together was one that they would both try to erase from their memories.

"I could never have done this without you," said Aron as they hugged good-bye.

"Nor I without you," replied Jakob. "And it was because of Levi that I knew we had to get away. It was his example in standing up for himself, and then his death, that made me want to get away before it was too late. It was Levi's courage that we have to thank for being here," he added quietly.

"The big challenge now will be to not let hatred rule our lives," Aron said. "If we do, we'll be no better than the Nazis."

Jakob nodded and smiled. "After I take care of Ivan, I will make sure to remember that."

PART
FOUR

Chapter 33

May 10, 1945

When Jakob arrived in Budapest and stood on the temporary platform beside the train, he found it difficult not to feel angry. All around him the city was in ruins. The Southern train station had been destroyed during a final two-day battle between the Russian and Nazi troops, which was why the passengers had to disembark several blocks away from the station.

He looked around, trying to get his bearings. Down the hill, in the distance, he could see the gray waters of the Danube and the ruins of the once-majestic Chain Bridge. He had learned at the refugee camp that all the bridges spanning the river within the boundaries of Budapest had been blown up by the retreating German army.

Jakob pulled a piece of paper from his pocket and read the address that had been given to him, along with some pocket money, at the

The view of Budapest when he finally reached the city filled Jakob with despair. The city was in ruins, its connecting bridges blown up by the retreating Nazis.

refugee camp. It was the location of a Red Cross compound where homeless refugees could go for shelter until they found new lodgings. He hesitated. Was he really homeless? He turned in the direction of his old neighborhood.

Though he could have easily jumped on a streetcar, he chose to walk. It was another sunny spring day, and after the long train ride he was eager to stretch his legs. He was curious to see everything along the way, what had been destroyed and what remained standing. It was a long walk, and after a few blocks he wished that he had taken the streetcar instead. So many signposts of his old life were missing, replaced by gaping caverns or piles of rubble that he had to pick his way around.

Yet there were also signs of hope. Amid the wreckage of one street stood a solitary café, intact, with its outdoor patio full of patrons sipping their espressos, talking, and smiling – as if the war had never happened. Farther over, the sweet scent of lilacs from a bush in full bloom filled the air. The joyful chatter of children in a schoolyard greeted him around one corner.

As he neared his street, Jakob's heart began to pound. What would he find? What if Mother opened the door to his knock? What if Father were sitting in his favorite easy chair, the newspaper opened in front of him? What if right now Magda were bending over a steaming pot of soup in the kitchen? What if all his fears had been unfounded? He began to run.

As soon as he turned the final corner, he stopped dead in his tracks. Most of the chestnut and sycamore trees were gone. Only a few burned tree trunks stood pitifully pointing at the sky. And there, where his apartment building used to be, was nothing but a pile of bricks. Nothing of the former structure remained standing. Tears of disappointment and frustration stung Jakob's eyes. How could he have been so foolish as to hope, even for a moment? He turned his back on the wreckage and headed slowly toward the address of the Red Cross compound.

Chapter 34

Jakob stood in the Red Cross food line waiting impatiently for his turn. The rich aroma of bean stew, fresh bread, and smoked meat tantalized his taste buds and made his mouth water. He still couldn't believe that at each meal he was given enough food to fill his belly. How different this food line was from the one composed of disheartened skeletons at Auschwitz. The voices here were animated and hopeful. There was even the occasional sound of laughter. Jakob realized how long it had been since he had heard that sound. The light, carefree melody of uninhibited laughter.

He himself did not feel like laughing and wondered if he ever would again. His family had been destroyed. He had no home. But for now, he had his mission. He was set on finding Ivan. Beyond that he had no plans. Beyond that he could see no purpose in his life. Occasionally he did odd jobs. There was plenty of work to be found these days with all the rebuilding. But mostly he wandered the streets, looking at the faces of people passing by, looking for someone he knew. He had revisited all their old haunts, those still left standing, but thus far without success.

At last it was his turn. He reached out his hands and gratefully accepted the full bowl of beans from the man with the ladle on the other side of the massive pot. The accompanying smile on the man's face was almost as welcome as the food. "I wish you a good appetite," the man said in a friendly voice. How different from the bitter curse of the Kapos. Tears of gratitude sprang to Jakob's eyes and he moved on. He cried too easily these days. Every gentle word or kind gesture still came as an unexpected surprise, a rare gift.

The next day he was back in line. The late afternoon sun's rays cast an amber glow over the long line of hungry men and women. Jakob's eyes were downcast, to avoid its glare. He shuffled slowly after the feet in front of him. He knew when it was time to look up and stretch out his hands by the waft of fragrant steam in his face. As he lifted his head, his eyes locked with those of the young man serving today's fare.

It was Ivan.

In an instant Jakob was behind the narrow table separating them. He barreled into Ivan, knocking the bowl from his hand, knocking him to the ground. Jakob had not yet fully regained his muscles or his weight, but the force of the impact, propelled by months of pent-up anger, left Ivan splayed on the pavement. Jakob was immediately on top of him, straddling Ivan, punching him in the face.

Blood spurted from Ivan's nose. Arms wrapped around Jakob. Hands grabbed his arms. Strangers pulled him off Ivan. Angry shouts exploded around him, but Jakob had ears only for Ivan's voice. He had eyes only for Ivan.

Once freed from Jakob, Ivan staggered to his feet.

"What are you doing?" Ivan shouted. "Are you crazy? Don't you recognize me? Don't you know who I am? I'm your friend Ivan. Why are you fighting me?"

"You are not my friend!" Jakob spit out the words. "You betrayed me. You killed my parents. You destroyed my family. You sent me to the concentration camp. I will make you pay. It's your turn to suffer now." Jakob shouted, and struggled to free himself from the vice-like grip of the man holding him.

"Hendrik, listen to me," pleaded Ivan. "Look at me. I am not who you think I am."

"I know who you are. You are a Nazi. And I am not Hendrik. My name is Jakob."

He flailed, desperate, futile. He had to punish Ivan.

"Jakob, then," Ivan said. "What does it matter? I'm still your friend. I never stopped being your friend."

"You are no friend of mine," Jakob's words and voice dripped with disgust. "A friend wouldn't have stood by and done nothing when I was taken captive and carted off to a concentration camp. A friend wouldn't have gone to report my parents so that they too would be arrested. A friend wouldn't have caused my family to die." Jakob's voice trembled and faded as he uttered the last words. Tears spilled down his cheeks. He didn't care. So what if Ivan saw him crying. Let Ivan get a small glimpse of the suffering he had caused.

There was a heavy moment of silence following Jakob's words. The crowd of onlookers stopped talking. Even the pigeons ceased their cooing. They all waited for Ivan's response.

"I did not cause your family to die," said Ivan at last, his voice barely above a whisper. "Your parents, your aunt Mimi and cousin Lilly, even your housekeeper, are all alive. I helped to save their lives."

Chapter 35

Jakob and Ivan sat in a café on the Buda side of the Danube. They faced each other across a small round table, their knees almost touching. Jakob had no clear recollection as to how they'd gotten there. At Ivan's words, he had gone limp in the arms of the strangers, stunned by what he had just heard. His family alive! Saved by Ivan? He hadn't understood back out in the street, and he still didn't understand now. But there had been a sincerity in Ivan's eyes that had momentarily calmed his anger. In that brief interval, Ivan convinced the men restraining Jakob that he could handle his friend. Somehow Ivan got Jakob inside this café, where they could talk more privately.

Jakob waited impatiently for Ivan's explanation. He sat straight and stiff on the small wrought-iron chair, refusing to allow either his posture or his heart to display any trust in Ivan. Ivan fidgeted and dabbed at his nose with a bloodstained handkerchief. He did not look at Jakob until after the waitress deposited a small cup of coffee in front of each of them. Jakob placed three cubes of sugar, a luxury, into his. Ivan preferred his black. He took a short sip and cleared his throat.

"That day in the ghetto," Ivan began. "I'm very sorry that things happened the way they did. I understand why you would be upset with me." Ivan looked down at his coffee cup and turned it slowly between his fingers. "I'm sorry that I said nothing in your defense at the time. But I couldn't. I was too stunned." Jakob's eyes glared at those words. He clenched his fists and leaned forward as if to speak, but Ivan, sensing the sudden change in Jakob, held up his hand, stopping him.

"Please, let me explain," Ivan continued, his eyes pleading. "I want you to understand what happened, what it was like for me. When you said that you were Jewish, I was shocked. I couldn't believe that it was true. You were my best friend. I guess I thought that I knew everything about you. It took me a minute to realize that of course you could never have told me you were Jewish. After all, my father was in the Arrow Cross." Ivan paused as if expecting some sort of response, but Jakob sat immobile, waiting to hear again those amazing words – that his family was alive.

"I had never really understood what it meant to be Jewish," Ivan continued. "Not till that day when my father took me to the ghetto and I saw how he treated Jews. I hadn't realized how the Jews had been forced to live by the Nazis and the Arrow Cross. Until that day,

Jew was just a word spoken with disdain. But seeing the ghetto," Ivan shook his head and shuddered at the memory, "I knew immediately that it was wrong to treat people like that. I realized how wrong I had been to want to join the Arrow Cross and be like my father. I only thought of holding a gun in my hands and having an adventure. For me, it was just another game. I never asked myself if what the Arrow Cross did was wrong.

"At the first building in the ghetto where we stopped, my father and his men forced several people onto a waiting truck, beating and kicking them to hurry them along. I grabbed at Father's arm and yelled at him to stop, but he shoved me away. He yelled back at me in return. 'I thought you were a man!' he said. 'You want to be an Arrow Cross soldier? Well here, do your part.' And he handed me a club.

"I felt horrible. Father was looking at his men who were nodding and smiling their approval. And then I saw a look in Father's eyes as he grabbed the next person." Ivan shook his head. "I don't think I will ever forget it. I was frightened. I realized that there was nothing I could do. Not then. It was clear that he was trying to impress his men and me. Nothing I said or did would have any effect in front of his men.

"So I pretended to go along. I waved my club around but made sure I never actually hit anyone. I even yelled a couple of times at the frightened people. I hated myself for doing it." Ivan paused and rubbed his forehead as if trying to erase the memory. "I kept telling myself that it was only for that day. I realized that I might never make my father see how wrong he was. He was too deeply involved. But I knew I had you to talk to. I was sure you would understand. We always understood each other."

Ivan looked into Jakob's eyes, searching for that understanding now. But Jakob still sat rigid, not allowing himself to relent, to soften, to show any sign of emotion. Not yet. Not until he heard more. For too long in Jakob's mind, Ivan had been a traitor to their friendship. He wasn't going to let go of that so easily. For the first time, Jakob was glad of the training he had received during those treacherous hours of roll call. He knew how to remain immobile regardless of what happened around him.

Ivan sighed and carried on. "I imagined coming home at the end of the day and telling you about what I had witnessed. I imagined the shock in your eyes. I imagined we would run away or somehow secretly work toward helping the people in the ghetto. I imagined us sabotaging the Arrow Cross, stealing their weapons and ammunition, doing whatever it took to undermine what they were doing. It was the only way I could cope with what was happening around me. I was getting quite carried away with all the planning. And then suddenly there you were." Ivan took a slow sip of his coffee.

"I didn't see you at first. I was hiding in the doorway of the next building, hoping to stay out of the way so they would forget about me and not make me do anything. And then I heard your voice. I recognized it at once. But what you said made no sense to me. You said that you were not Hendrik, that your name was Jakob. That you were a Jew. I didn't understand." Again Ivan looked directly at Jakob, asking with his eyes if Jakob understood. And still Jakob remained silent, unmoved.

Chapter 36

A waitress intruded on their silence and asked if they would like anything else. Ivan, noticing that Jakob had barely touched his coffee, waved her away.

"I didn't understand then, but I do now," Ivan continued as soon as she left. "I know your father forced you and your mother never to talk about your Jewish past. Your mother told me."

Your mother told me. The words rang loud in Jakob's mind.

"My mother told you?" he asked before he could think or stop himself. "*When* did she tell you?" His voice was barely above a whisper. Ivan drew his brows together, trying to remember.

"I'm not sure. About a week after you were captured. Once we had a chance to talk about all that had happened."

A week later! If Mother was alive a week later, if she was talking with Ivan, then maybe it was true that she was still alive. And the others. Jakob's shoulders sagged and his features softened. He let out a deep breath. He downed his coffee in a couple of gulps. Encouraged by the change, Ivan continued.

"Back in the ghetto, I was taken totally by surprise. But when you said that you were a Jew, I knew without a doubt that everything my father stood for was wrong. You were my friend. The fact that you were Jewish didn't make you a different person from the best friend I had known for years. I *knew* you. It took me a few moments to understand what was happening, to collect myself. By then it was almost too late."

Despite what Ivan was saying, Jakob's anger surged again as he relived those horrible moments. At the same time, though, there was that word: "almost." It made his heart beat faster.

"What do you mean by 'almost'?" Jakob asked. "It *was* too late. My cousin Gabor was dead. My cousin Lilly, my aunt, and I were taken prisoners. My parents were about to be arrested. And you did nothing. You just left us to our fate and ran off to do your father's bidding."

"No, you don't understand," Ivan shook his head. "When my father asked me to go back to our street and alert the guards, I knew that it was my opportunity to get away. It was the only chance I had to help.

"Remember what Brother Ferenc told us at the beginning of the school year?" Ivan went on, "He told us that to become men, we have to make our own choices. Well, I knew I didn't want to be like my father.

185

"I decided not to follow his orders. I did not alert the guards. I did not go back to your apartment. Instead, I hurried to the monastery to see Brother Ferenc. I explained to him what was happening and sought his advice. Without hesitation, he told me to bring your parents to the monastery to be hidden until we could come up with a better plan.

"I ran like crazy to reach your parents. I was so scared that the patrols would receive my father's instructions and that your parents wouldn't get away in time. Also, I knew they couldn't be seen leaving *after* I went into the building. I had to be able to tell my father that they were already gone by the time I got there."

"What did you do?" asked Jakob, suddenly caught up in the drama of Ivan's account. He involuntarily clutched at Ivan's arm as if willing him to succeed.

"Remember that passageway we found years ago, between our coal cellar and the one in the next building? We took that route and then snuck out into the back alley. Your mother insisted that your housekeeper, Magda, go with them."

Jakob pictured his mother and father and Magda bent over, hurrying through the narrow, dark and dusty tunnel, emerging at the other end, disheveled and frightened.

"They hid in the monastery for about a week until Raoul Wallenberg arranged to make room for them in one of his protected houses. Brother Ferenc knew Wallenberg well and contacted him as soon as your parents were safe in the monastery. Neither the Nazis nor the Arrow Cross were allowed to search through any of Wallenberg's buildings."

"Who is Raoul Wallenberg?" Jakob frowned at the mention of the unfamiliar name.

"He is a Swedish diplomat who was working to save the lives of many Jews. Mr. Wallenberg managed to get them false documents, which stated that they were under the protection of the Swedish government," Ivan added.

"After your parents reached the monastery, I backtracked as quickly as I could and pretended to carry out Father's orders. Of course, when the guards knocked on your parents' door, there was nobody there. Father never suspected that I had anything to do with their disappearance.

"There was a whole network set in motion by Wallenberg to protect as many Jews as possible. He saved thousands of Hungarian Jews from the camps and death. I soon learned that he wasn't the only one helping. There were many other organizations and individuals who helped to hide Jews however they could. Brother Ferenc was one of them as well."

"Brother Ferenc?" asked Jakob, though he was not surprised by the revelation. "Yes, it would be the kind of thing he would do. I had wondered that day in class if he suspected my secret."

"He did suspect that you were Jewish. He told me that when

I went to seek his help," said Ivan. "But of course he couldn't say anything to you in school."

Ivan continued his story. "After I took your parents to the monastery, I started working for Wallenberg as well. At home, I pretended that I was still interested in joining the Arrow Cross, so Father would trust me. Through Father, I was able to gain information to pass on to Mr. Wallenberg, who used it to protect the people working with him. Living a double life like that proved to be quite challenging for me at times. But it was exciting, and it also helped me to feel a little less guilty about not being able to help you."

"So my parents *are* alive?" asked Jakob, most intent on hearing his parents' story.

"Yes, of course they are," nodded Ivan. "They have their own apartment now. I will take you there. They have been desperately trying to find out whether you were still alive. That's one of the reasons I have been helping out with the Red Cross, to try to find you. Each day I made sure I was posted to a different location."

A combination of relief and shame flooded through Jakob for having doubted Ivan's friendship. He slumped forward and buried his face in his hands. "How could I have been so wrong about you?" he whispered. Slowly, he lifted his head and looked at Ivan with new eyes. The hated enemy he had imagined for so long had rematerialized as his friend again. He had turned out to be a friend more loyal and heroic than Jakob could ever have imagined.

"I should never have doubted you," Jakob said quietly. "I'm so sorry for the horrible things I thought about you. The whole time at the concentration camp I thought you had betrayed my family – that you were responsible for their deaths. I wanted revenge. All I wanted was to live long enough to pay you back for what you had done. Can you forgive me?" Jakob's shoulders shook and he again pressed his face into his hands. Tears leaked from between his fingers. Remorse replaced the anger that had been his companion for so long.

He felt a gentle hand on his shoulder.

"Of course I forgive you," said Ivan. "But I too need forgiveness. Before all of this, I know I was the driving force behind our attempts to join the Arrow Cross. I should have known better, but I willingly blinded myself to the truth – until that day in the ghetto when it was impossible not to see the truth. I too, am sorry. I'm so sorry for all you had to suffer."

Jakob looked up and smiled through his tears. He reached across the narrow table and placed his hand on Ivan's shoulder. "I forgive you," said Jakob.

Chapter 37

Jakob and Ivan sat and smiled at each other for a long time. They were friends again – the best of friends.

The waitress came and removed their empty coffee cups. Suddenly, Jakob was ravenous. He had never received or eaten the dinner he had stood in line for. He was anxious to see his parents again, but there were still questions he wanted answered and things he wanted to tell Ivan. They ordered soup and crêpes and, when the waitress left, resumed their conversation.

"Tell me what happened to you," Ivan said softly. "You mentioned a concentration camp. Which one were you in? We have heard dreadful accounts of what happened in the death camps. Such cruelty, and on such a mass scale is – it's incomprehensible."

Jakob was quiet for a long time, not knowing how to begin. Then slowly he rolled up his left sleeve and showed Ivan the numbers tattooed there.

"I was in Auschwitz," he said barely above a whisper.

"Auschwitz," Ivan echoed the word. "I've heard it was one of the worst of the camps. Thousands of people were sent to the gas chambers there."

When Jakob remained silent, Ivan said, "You know, Wallenberg and his men tried to rescue you, as well. But you seemed to have vanished in the trains. They managed to get your Aunt Mimi and Lilly off the train. But the guards couldn't find you."

"Aunt Mimi and Lilly are alive? But I don't understand how that could be. The last time I saw them, they were forced to leave the train. They were taken off to be shot."

"No. You are mistaken," Ivan shook his head. "After Brother Ferenc told Wallenberg what had happened with you and your family, Mr. Wallenberg immediately set out to rescue you and your aunt and cousin from the trains. He found out which train you three had been put on and raced with a truck to catch up before it crossed the border into Poland. He managed to block its progress by straddling the tracks where it crossed a road just before the border. Mr. Wallenberg had false documents for about twenty people on that train. You, your aunt, and your cousin were among them. They found your Aunt Mimi and Lilly. But the guards insisted that they couldn't find you. They went from car to car shouting your name to no avail. They ended up having to leave without you."

Jakob stared wide-eyed at Ivan, remembering. The cramped train, his knothole, the vision of Aunt Mimi and Lilly, in his green and orange striped sweater, being led away at gunpoint. At the time, he had turned away and closed his eyes. He had covered his ears. He had refused to watch or hear anything, because he thought they were about to be shot like the other prisoners had been at the previous stop.

And then he remembered that, though his hands were covering his ears, he *had* heard the muffled sounds of the car door opening – the unintelligible hum of voices, faint behind the pulsing of his own blood through his veins. Could it be that the guards had been looking for him? That they had yelled out his name? If he had heard his name being called, he might have escaped the horrors of the last six months.

Jakob's body began to shake uncontrollably. He clasped a hand over his mouth to keep from crying out loud. The tears streamed down his face, tears of sorrow for all he had suffered, tears of relief that Aunt Mimi and Lilly were alive.

Ivan had shifted his chair around so that he was beside Jakob. He put an arm around his friend.

"It's all right," Ivan said softly, hugging Jakob. "It's all over now. You are safe, and soon you will see your family again." Gradually, Jakob regained his composure and Ivan moved his chair back to face Jakob. Their soup arrived.

"We were given soup at the camp," Jakob began, after savoring his first mouthful, "but it was nothing like this." As they ate, Jakob told Ivan about his arrival at Auschwitz, about the barracks, the Kapo, the awful living conditions, and the killings that had surrounded him. He told him about Aron and Levi, about Levi's death, and finally the story of his and Aron's dangerous escape.

As he talked and saw the tears well in Ivan's eyes, Jakob felt the burden of the last seven months ease. For the first time in a long time, he began to think that maybe it was possible to live again. That there would be a future for him. His longing for revenge had been replaced with a longing for life.

Chapter 38

It was dark outside when they left the café. Ivan had told Jakob that his parents had moved back to the Pest side of the Danube, close to the area where they had lived before the war. It was a mild May evening, and after a streetcar took them down the hill close to the river, the boys decided to continue on foot.

They walked along the ramparts, frequently detouring around the rubble of bombed-out buildings. Suddenly, Jakob was not in such a big rush to see his parents. Though Ivan assured him that they had forgiven him for blurting out their secret and were only concerned for his well-being, Jakob couldn't imagine that they wouldn't be upset over what he had done. Perhaps they blamed him for having destroyed the life that they had worked so hard to establish. Especially Father. How would Father react to seeing him again? Jakob's steps slowed as they approached the makeshift pontoon bridge that temporarily spanned the river where the Margit Bridge had once stood.

"Where are you and your parents living?" he asked Ivan. For the first time since encountering Ivan, Jakob thought of Sergeant Biro. What was he doing now that the Arrow Cross had been outlawed and the Nazis driven from the country? Accepting Ivan as a friend again was fine, but Jakob knew that he could never face Sergeant Biro now. "I went back to our old apartment when I first returned, only to find that it had been completely destroyed," Jakob said.

Ivan bit his bottom lip, hesitating for a moment. "I don't know where my parents are living," he said slowly, "or for that matter, whether they are living at all." When he saw Jakob's shocked expression, he added, "It's all right. It was my decision to stay. When the German army retreated before the advance of the Russians in February, many Arrow Cross soldiers and their families left with the Germans. They retreated to countries still occupied by Germany, or to Germany itself. They knew that their days here were numbered and that their lives were in danger. People wanted revenge.

"My parents were among the first to leave," Ivan continued. "They packed up their things quickly and ordered me to do the same. I told them I wasn't going with them. I confessed to Father that I despised what he had done during the war, that I had worked against the Nazis behind his back. He was furious and I thought he was going to strike me, knock me out, and carry me with them, but Mother stopped

Ivan and Jakob passed the rubble of bombed out shops and apartments on their way to find Jakob's parents.

him. In the commotion, I left. No one came after me." Ivan sighed. "I wish our parting hadn't been like that. I would have liked to have said good-bye, especially to Mother. But there wasn't much else I could do at the time. There was so much turmoil, and decisions needed to be made so quickly. Maybe one day everyone will move freely again between countries, and I can try to find them," Ivan said hopefully. "At least I would like to know that Mother is all right." This time it was Jakob who put his arms around Ivan's shoulders.

"So where do you live now?" Jakob asked after a moment. Ivan smiled, and there was a mischievous look in his eye.

"I live with your parents, of course. We can finally be true brothers. And by the way, since you have revealed yourself to be Jakob, that is how they refer to you now. Though officially you are still Hendrik Varga."

They had reached the temporary Margit Bridge and crossed over to Pest. Though many soldiers still walked in the streets, these were Russian and Hungarian soldiers. There were no patrols to fear now at either end of the bridge. After a couple of blocks, Ivan led Jakob off the main thoroughfare and onto a narrow side street where he stopped in front of a gray stone apartment building.

"This is it," he said, spreading his arms wide. "This is where we live now. Not quite as luxurious as the old building, but given the circumstances, it's not too bad. There are many people still waiting for apartments." Ivan led the way up to the third floor, halfway around the courtyard balcony, and knocked on a faded green door.

Jakob's heart pounded. For an instant he doubted everything that Ivan had told him. What if this was a trap? But then the door opened and his mother was standing in the warm glow of the kitchen behind her.

"Ivan, we were beginning to worry about you," she started to say, wiping her hands on her apron. Then she looked up and saw who was standing there beside Ivan. Her hands flew to her chest and she gasped. In the next instant, her arms were around Jakob. She began to laugh and cry at the same time, calling loudly for Father, for Aunt Mimi, for Lilly, for Magda, for everyone to come and see who had finally returned home.

After the joyous welcome had died down, Jakob stood awkwardly in the kitchen, unsure of what to say or do. To him, it seemed impossible that his parents did not blame him, did not resent the dramatic change he had brought about in their lives. Mother ushered him into the living room, where Jakob noted the confined space, the worn and faded furniture. All of the luxuries from their previous home – the crystal ornaments, the books, the paintings – were gone.

Mother and Father brought in extra chairs from the kitchen and everyone sat in a small circle, eager to hear his story of survival and eager to tell their own. Jakob heard all over again the story of Mother and Father's frightened flight from the apartment, of Brother Ferenc's selfless assistance. He heard of Aunt Mimi's and Lilly's timely liberation from the train bound for Auschwitz, of how Mr. Wallenberg had taken them to one of his safe houses where they remained until the Russians drove the Nazis out of Budapest. Jakob's parents and Aunt Mimi each spoke of their appreciation for Ivan and of his role in saving their lives. They talked of the positive things that had happened and, for the time being, made no mention of losses and deaths.

Jakob, in turn, tried his best to avoid describing the hardships he had endured at Auschwitz. Mother and Father, Aunt Mimi, and Lilly had suffered enough. He did not want to burden them with the pain of his own sufferings. Instead he spoke mainly of his friendships with Aron and Levi. He told them of their Hanukkah celebration, of Levi singing for the Nazi officers, of his and Aron's escape, and their being found by the Russian Allies. Occasionally Jakob caught Ivan's eye, but his friend gave no indication that he noticed the differences between this account and the one told in the coffee shop. Even with the many gaps in Jakob's story, the time passed quickly, and it was well past midnight when they finally parted for the night.

As Jakob headed toward the room he was to share with Ivan, Father stopped him. The time had come, Jakob knew, to talk about what he had done. He bowed his head, unable to meet his father's gaze as he tried to find the right words with which to begin his apology. Suddenly, Jakob felt his father's strong hands grip his shoulders. Jakob looked up into his father's eyes.

"Jakob," his father said, "look at you. You left as a boy, and came back a man. Even so," Father cleared his throat, "even when you were a boy, I should have trusted you more. As you grew, I should have trusted you to understand why it was necessary for us to change our lives. I laid a heavy burden upon you when I asked you to forget the past. To never speak about it. My fear of being discovered blinded me to everything else. If we had talked more openly, perhaps all this suffering could have been avoided." Father's voice cracked and there were tears in his eyes. "I am so very sorry. Will you forgive me?" he asked, his voice barely above a whisper.

Jakob, too choked up to speak, nodded as he embraced his father. "I too am sorry," he managed to say after a while. "When I went to the ghetto, I wasn't thinking of the consequences of my actions. I was so angry about what I saw in the ghetto."

"Everything will be all right," Father said, rubbing Jakob's back, "now that you are here."

Chapter 39

It wasn't as simple as Father had suggested. Everything wasn't all right. Gabor was still dead and, as Jakob soon discovered, so was his Uncle Peter. After the war, Aunt Mimi learned that he had been transferred from the labor camp to Auschwitz and killed shortly after the Nazis invaded Hungary.

Aunt Mimi had embraced Jakob that first night of his arrival, and told him that she did not blame him for what happened to Gabor. "He was always defiant and spoke his mind, just like his father," she had said. "After the Nazi invasion, I feared for his life every minute of every day." Though her words were kind, the look in her eyes was distant. Over the course of the next few days, Jakob noticed that her proud bearing was gone. There was an agitation, a restlessness about her that Jakob did not recognize.

Lilly, on the other hand, though still very quiet, now seemed calm.

She had begun to put on some weight and no longer looked like she might get knocked over by the slightest breeze. Every time their eyes met, she smiled at Jakob.

All had been forgiven, yet Jakob sensed an unacknowledged tension in the air as they went about their daily business. As Ivan had told Jakob, his parents still kept their Christian identities.

"Just because the Nazis are gone and the Arrow Cross is no longer in power doesn't mean that the hearts of the Hungarian people are no longer racist," Father had explained. "There is still a lot of anti-Semitism around. And no one knows what the future holds here in Hungary. I am fortunate to still have my job, where I am known as Janos Varga. We will keep our last name as Varga. We can call you Jakob at home, but to the outside world you are still officially Hendrik," he told his son.

Mother was clearly pleased to share their apartment with Aunt Mimi and Lilly. But Aunt Mimi herself was not content with the current set-up. "I don't belong here," she would mutter as she restlessly paced the living room. She was a seamstress by profession, but the shop where she had worked before the invasion had been bombed. Her sewing machine had been confiscated along with her other belongings. "I need to make a living and have something worthwhile to do," she told Jakob one day. "Something more than volunteering for the Jewish relief organization. This just reminds me of how much our lives have been forever altered."

Jakob understood what she meant. He too felt restless and out of place. A couple of days after his return home, Ivan had suggested that Jakob accompany him on his temporary work assignment. "School isn't going to start up again till September, so I have been joining the crews clearing away all the rubble on the streets. We can just turn up at a site and get paid at the end of the day for our labor. It will be a good way to rebuild those muscles," Ivan had said with a smile.

Jakob went with Ivan but found that lifting the heavy boulders was too similar to the hard labor he had done at Auschwitz. Every bent form reminded him of his fellow inmates and the grueling conditions under which they had worked in the camps. The blisters that quickly formed on his hands brought to mind the suffering they had all endured at the prison camp. By mid-day he was ready to quit. Ivan, who relished both the physical exertion and the camaraderie between the workers, tried to understand.

Jakob discovered that even though Ivan was still a good friend, their different experiences during the last several months had created a chasm between them. Apart from his friendship with Aron and Levi and the knowledge he had gained about the Jewish faith, Jakob's life had been pure misery. Pain and death had been his daily companions. The heavy labor he had been forced to do had only benefited the hated enemy.

Ivan, on the other hand, had continued to live in relative comfort with his family. Though daily exposing himself to danger as he helped in the underground efforts to save the lives of Jews, his work was both exciting and rewarding. He had not lost his love of adventure. Ivan was eager to help with the rebuilding of their once-beautiful Budapest. He wanted to help transform it back into a city where all could move about freely and live in harmony.

Jakob, like Aunt Mimi, found it difficult to see beyond the debris – not just of the buildings but also of people's lives. Now that he was home, images of Auschwitz haunted him day and night. He jumped whenever a voice was raised or an order sharply given. Smoke rising from piles of burning debris reminded him of the stacks of smoldering corpses that he had passed daily at the camp. At night his dreams were filled with people being shot or dying. He would awaken to the phantom stench of the gas chambers, and would jump out of bed to open his windows wide.

It was only by immersing himself in books, in learning and discussions, that Jakob found relief. He spent hours at the library reading about the long history of the Jewish people. He learned about the persecution of the Jews over the centuries and of their constant triumph over adversity. He visited Brother Ferenc frequently and talked with him of the many commandments he had discussed with Levi. Brother Ferenc often pointed out the similarities between Jewish and Christian values. "Jesus was Jewish after all," smiled Brother Ferenc. "Our values stem from the same roots."

Encouraged by his remarks, Jakob told Brother Ferenc of his intention to have a bar mitzvah. "Yes," Brother Ferenc nodded, agreeing. "Your Jewish identity is in your blood. That will never change," he said. "It is right that you acknowledge your identity as you take steps toward the responsibilities of manhood. But remember that this is only the beginning. It is the first step on the path that you have chosen to follow. And remember as you travel along your path that my door is always open to you."

Jakob learned of a small synagogue where people went to pray and to study. It was near their new apartment and had survived the carnage of the war. There he met the rabbi and made arrangements with him to continue the studies he'd begun with Levi. He also learned Hebrew so that he could read the prayers and chant passages from the Torah.

It was on his way home from the synagogue in mid-July that he bumped into Aunt Mimi sitting on a park bench in the shade of a towering chestnut tree. He was surprised to see her cheeks flushed and a smile lighting up her face. He sat down beside her. "I have booked passage on a ship bound for Canada for Lilly and me," she announced with excitement. "We have our visas and will be leaving in two months. Your father has offered to pay for our move."

"To Canada?" Jakob knew little about Canada except that it was one of the Allied countries that had helped to liberate Europe.

"Yes. It is a vast country across the ocean, far from all this." She waved her arms at the ruins that surrounded the small green oasis.

"They are accepting Jewish refugees, like us, who have lost everything in the war. We will start over, Lilly and I. They say that Canada is a free land where all people are treated with respect. The people at the Red Cross said that I should be able to find work there as a seamstress. We will be arriving in a city called Halifax and will be helped by the Jewish agency to relocate from there."

"Canada!" Jakob said again with wonder. He had not thought of the possibility of living somewhere other than Hungary. His parents had discussed it but had decided to stay in Budapest. He wished suddenly that he too were going. A fresh start sounded very appealing to him.

"Maybe," said Aunt Mimi as if reading his thoughts, "when you are a bit older, after Lilly and I are established, you can come and visit. Maybe you can even stay and live with us for a while."

"Yes," nodded Jakob, smiling now too, "I think that I would like that very much."

Epilogue

August 28, 1945

Jakob stood for the first time in front of the congregation of the synagogue. With trembling fingers he unrolled the scroll of the Torah that had been placed before him by the rabbi. He found the place where his bar mitzvah passage was located and began to chant.

Jakob raised his head without stopping the flow of the Hebrew words. He had committed them to memory weeks ago. He looked out at the small gathering before him. Father and Mother watched him proudly. Aunt Mimi and Lilly were seated next to them. They would be leaving for their new home in Canada before the week was out. He scanned the meager assembly of Jewish survivors in the congregation. For a moment he let his imagination take over. Filling the empty spaces, he saw the faces of all those who had perished in the concentration camps, the ghettos, on the death marches. A vast multitude! And there in their midst stood Levi, swaying gently to the rhythm of Jakob's words.

For a second, Jakob rested his eyes on Brother Ferenc and Ivan where they stood at the back of the assembly. Their eyes locked as Jakob finished the passage.

Today I have given you the choice between life and death, between blessings and curses. Now I call on heaven and earth to witness the choice you make. Oh, that you would choose life, so that you and your descendants might live!

(Deut. Ch. 30)

Kathy's father, Frigyes Porscht, (whose childhood inspired this book) holds his smiling daughter in 1953.

The author was reunited with her father in 2000.

Acknowledgments

I am greatly indebted to the many people who helped to make this book possible.

Foremost of these is Frigyes Porscht who, in sharing with me his traumatic experiences as a young adult during the Holocaust, first planted the seeds of this story in my mind.

Margie Wolfe of Second Story Press, who saw potential in the story and who helped me to focus and guide my initial ideas toward a meaningful end.

Juszi and Erzsi Szirtes, who kindly shared their own stories with me, revisiting a painful past, and who gave me permission to incorporate any aspect of their ordeal into my book.

The City of Ottawa Arts Council for their financial support.

My friend and mentor, Paddy Dupuis, who as my foremost critic helped me to mold the story into its initial presentable stage.

The staff at Second Story Press, who assisted me in all aspects of the production.

Sarah Swartz, my editor, who once again helped with her timely advice and persevered through fine-tuning *The Choice* into a compelling story.

And finally, my family, both immediate and extended, who gave me the freedom and space to write and encouraged me throughout the lengthy process of bringing the book to completion.

Photo Credits

About the Author

Kathy Clark is the author of *Guardian Angel House*, an OLA Red Maple Award finalist inspired by her mother and aunt's lives as Jewish children hidden from the Nazis. *The Choice* is inspired by her father's experiences, also in the Holocaust. Kathy lives in Kanata, Ontario and was raised by her mother and a loving stepfather. She learned of the events described in this book as an adult when she became reacquainted with her dad.

We Are Their Voice
Young People Respond to the Holocaust
Kathy Kacer
ISBN: 978-1-897187-96-8
$14.95

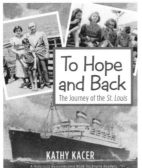

To Hope and Back
Kathy Kacer
ISBN: 978-1-897187-96-8
$14.95

Shanghai Escape
Kathy Kacer
ISBN: 978-1-927583-10-4
$14.95

The Holocaust Remembrance Series for Young Readers

Guardian Angel House
Kathy Clark
ISBN: 978-1-897187-58-6
$14.95

The Diary of Laura's Twin
Kathy Kacer
ISBN: 978-1-897187-39-5
$14.95

Hana's Suitcase
Karen Levine
ISBN: 978-1-896764-55-9
$16.95

Hiding Edith - *A True Story*
Kathy Kacer
ISBN: 978-1-897187-06-7
$14.95

The Underground Reporters
A True Story
Kathy Kacer
ISBN:
978-1-896764-85-6
$15.95

The Righteous Smuggler
Debbie Spring
ISBN:
978-1-896764-97-9
$9.95

Clara's War
Kathy Kacer
ISBN:
978-1-896764-42-9
$8.95

The Secret of Gabi's Dresser
Kathy Kacer
ISBN:
978-1-896764-15-3
$7.95

The Night Spies
Kathy Kacer
ISBN:
978-1-896764-70-2
$8.95